Helen supposed she was reasonably content with her marriage-that-was-no-marriage to Drew Lincoln—after six years she was used to it—but what about Drew? Having kept studiously out of her way wherever possible, suddenly he was always there, disturbing, overbearing, and—what? She couldn't possibly be finding him attractive after all this time, could she?

SENSATION

BY
CHARLOTTE LAMB

MILLS & BOON LIMITED
17–19 FOLEY STREET
LONDON W1A 1DR

*First published 1979
Australian copyright 1980
Philippine copyright 1980
This edition 1980*

© Charlotte Lamb 1979

ISBN 0 263 73198 7

Set in Linotype Plantin 11 on 12 pt.

*Made and printed in Great Britain by
Richard Clay (The Chaucer Press), Ltd., Bungay, Suffolk*

CHAPTER ONE

THEY met at Orly airport. Helen was following her porter when a small boy in a red terry shirt and shorts burst the balloon he was carrying. The bang sounded like gunfire. Security men raced towards the noise. Women gasped and swung round. The little boy began to wail and then everyone began to laugh as they realised what had really happened.

Helen was still smiling as she turned to walk after her porter. When hands seized her upper arms she looked up and stared incredulously. 'What are *you* doing here?'

He ran a hand through thick black hair, his brows raised. 'What are you?'

'On my way to Paris,' she returned, aware that some women nearby were staring at him and in a fashion with which she was all too horribly familiar. Drew always got looks like that. His height and air of lazy confidence, his hard good looks, the amused smile in the light grey eyes, always attracted female attention. He was accustomed to it, expected it, indeed, enjoyed it.

Although she was astonished to see him, it was apt that they should meet in an airport. For years they had passed each other in flight, coming and going, always in opposite directions. It was surprising that they had never met like this before, she decided, and partly because it gave her a little sting of pleasure to see him, partly because she was still amused by the little incident earlier with the boy and his balloon, she was more relaxed than she normally was in his company, her blue eyes returning the smile in his face.

'Where are you off to?' she asked him lightly.

'Paris,' he said, with a twist of the hard mouth.

Her face changed. 'I thought you were in Jamaica for another week.' A frown knit her brows. She had checked his schedule very carefully before she left London. Had she made a mistake for the first time? She was always so cautious, double-checking all his arrangements.

'I was,' he said drily, 'but I tied it up faster than I'd expected.' He glanced over his shoulder at where her porter was disappearing into the distance. 'Your luggage is making off at a rate of knots.'

'Oh,' she said on a little groan, biting her lip. He fell into step as she moved away and she gave him a worried look.

'Where's your luggage?'

'Meredith arrived with it on an earlier flight.'

'Of course.' The faint trace of sarcasm in her tone did not escape him. Drew had his life organised to a hair's breadth. He never did anything he could get someone else to do. He called it delegating. It meant that Drew could stroll as he pleased, unburdened with such things as luggage or responsibilities.

Now he was looking at her with a glinting little smile. With soft malice he asked her the question which he already knew was troubling her.

'Where are you staying?'

'The apartment,' she said, looking back at him with wary eyes. 'Where are you?' Please say a hotel, she thought, or one of your friends. Paris was crammed with his friends. Surely he must be going to one of them.

But he said softly, 'The apartment,' and there was a familiar curl of derision at his mouth. The situation was amusing him—she saw that. And it made her blood boil.

Faint colour crept into her cheeks. A line etched itself between her finely pencilled brows. She had, of course, suspected it. With Drew she always suspected the worst. But she had hoped otherwise. It was a situation she had always hoped to avoid. For years she had dovetailed their activities so that they rarely met and if they did spend time under one roof it was always with a number of guests to make it easy.

They were threading their way through crowds of people, Drew keeping pace with her easily, his long legs moving at her side in a graceful stroll. They made a striking couple, but of this Helen was unaware, her mind obsessed by the problem which had just been presented to her.

'Are you alone?' She would not normally have even hinted at that question, but in the circumstances she had to know if he had anyone with him. She was not staying in the apartment if he had a woman there.

'No,' he drawled, watching her out of the corner of his eyes, a gleam of masculine amusement in his face.

'Oh.' She flushed more deeply, her tone holding impatience, irritation. 'I wish you had let me know you'd changed your itinerary. Now I shall have to try to book into a hotel.'

'I don't see why.'

Helen almost never lost her temper, but she was close

to losing it now. The cool, composed face was filling with colour. 'You know perfectly well why! I don't give a damn how many mistresses you have, but you're not getting me to stay in the apartment while one of them is there!'

'Did I mention the sex of my guest?' He grinned down at her, teasing amusement in his face. 'I'm expecting Philip Cameron, actually.'

She felt a wave of sheer fury mounting to her head like the fumes of some potent drink. Her eyes flashed fire at him, their blue suddenly brilliant in the smooth oval of her face. Drew's eyes narrowed on her. She was always cool and polite with him and the unusual vivacity altered her whole face.

'That wasn't funny,' she snapped.

'Wasn't it?'

'You knew what I thought you meant.'

'Oh, I knew,' he drawled. 'It should teach you not to jump to conclusions.'

They had emerged into blinding sunlight. Helen's porter stood waiting with a long-suffering face. He opened his mouth to make some sarcastic comment, judging from his look, and Drew gave him a brief glance which shut his mouth and made him stand to attention. Not for the first time she found it infuriating that he should have this effect on people. For a lazily cool man he had a surprising ability to make people jump.

'I've a car waiting somewhere,' she said vaguely.

'Good, it can take me too,' Drew drawled.

Moments later they were speeding towards Paris, his long legs stretched out beside her, his hands jammed into his pockets, looking as though he were utterly relaxed, swaying with the motion of the car. Helen gave him an oblique look and found him watching her, an insolent smile in the grey eyes.

'You look very charming,' he told her, letting his gaze rove slowly from her classically cool features down her slender body in her grey suit to the long, slim legs.

'Thank you,' she said in a courteous voice, hoping she was concealing from him the effect he was having with that leisurely inspection.

'What are you going to Paris for?'

'Clothes,' she said succinctly. He liked her to dress well. He had always taken an interest in her clothes. She was, after all, window-dressing for him, on display whenever she was seen in public. It was part of their bargain.

'How's Stephen?' he asked.

'I wondered when you'd ask,' she returned tartly.

'I assumed he was well or you wouldn't have left him,' he retorted. 'I spoke to him on the phone two days ago and he seemed in great shape.'

She frowned. She had not been told he had rung. Before she could contemplate the implications of that, he asked: 'How are your parents?'

'Well,' she said.

The brevity ended that conversation. She turned her head to look out of the window, frowning. She could feel him watching her and it annoyed her. The only reason their marriage had worked so well was because they never met and she was disturbed to imagine them being alone for any time.

Six years ago when she left school she had been desperately bored. The life her parents wanted her to lead left her wanting to scream. She was the only child of wealthy parents. As far as they were concerned, her future was mapped out. When she could be found a suitable man, she would marry, and until that happened she was to be on display to attract a possible husband. They gave dinner parties for her, they took her to dances, they sent her to stay with friends. Helen found all this busy socialising tedious. Although her looks were outstanding, her remote manner froze men off and her mother was at her wits' end to know what to do with her.

'You're so tongue-tied. They said at that school that you were clever, but I don't see any signs of it,' said Leona, throwing up her hands. Leona adored parties, small talk, gossip. She could not understand her tall, slender blonde daughter. Helen was a great disappointment to her.

Grey was in the construction business. The lack of a son made him feel irritated whenever he set eyes on Helen. He urgently wanted to get her married and producing grandsons who could one day inherit his firm.

It was Grey who brought Drew Lincoln to the house. Drew was in the same business. He specialised in foreign contracts. He built roads and cities in developing countries. On one project he was working alongside Grey's firm and the two men had formed a friendship, a genial competitive friendship which would not stop at cutting each other's throats, all with a broad smile.

Helen had been present by accident, since her dinner date for the evening had cried off with an excuse she suspected to be fabricated. He had proposed to her the day before and she had politely turned him down.

Her parents had been expecting the proposal and had indicated to her that they wanted her to accept. In consequence, they had been furious with her. All day she had been receiving angry looks from them.

Her mother had shown less than her usual interest in what Helen wore that evening, merely giving her simple cream dinner dress a resigned glance. There were several other guests, all known to Helen, but it was Drew Lincoln who got the benefit of her mother's brightest smiles, her father's gruff badinage. Helen sat silent, listening.

'This lad's the worst ladykiller I ever met,' Grey had told another guest. 'Dynamite! I don't know how he ever finds time for work. Every time I see him, there's a different one on his arm. He gets 'em by the lorry load, I'd say.'

Helen had barely glanced at Drew. One look had told her enough. Tall, lithe, broad-shouldered, he had lounged in his chair, smiling indolently.

She had been seated opposite him at the table. Except when she was exchanging polite small talk with the people on each side of her, she remained largely silent, concentrating on the bowl of flowers in the centre of the table. Drew never spoke to her and she never looked at him.

After dinner her father had said tersely, 'Play something, Helen.' The other guests had murmured politely, little smiles on their faces, boredom in their eyes. Helen had sat down at the piano expressionlessly and played a bravura piece, all technique and no feeling, knowing it would impress by the sheer speed and agility of her fingers. She had accepted the surprised applause with a faint smile, her eyes veiled.

Grey then took his guests to admire the tropical flowers he kept in his overheated conservatory. They were his hobby, an expensive one which gave him a permanent spare-time occupation. Everyone had gone. Left alone, Helen had sighed with relief and let her hands drift into reverie, the reflective music of the Waldstein Sonata emerging. Grave, sonorous, it matched her mood. She stared vaguely at her own reflection in the deeply polished wood, a misty blur of gold and cream which was suddenly disturbed by another face. It appeared behind her, merging with her image, dark and predatory. A shiver ran down her back.

She looked round, her hands still, and Drew Lincoln regarded her with a trace of sardonic amusement. 'Very different,' he commented. 'Your audience seemed dazzled by the virtuoso stuff, though. Shrewd of you to guess they would be.'

'But not you?' she asked, sliding him a look from beneath her long, pale lashes.

He strolled forward and leaned on the piano, smiling. 'The technique was impressive, but it had no heart.'

'I didn't write the music,' she retorted.

'No,' he agreed. 'But you played it and from the disdainful little smile you gave them when they applauded, I suspect you despised them for enjoying it, even though you had deliberately chosen to play that particular piece. You were making a judgment about them, weren't you?'

'Do you really think they would have preferred the Beethoven?' she asked drily.

'I doubt it,' he agreed. 'It was your cleverness they applauded.'

'They would have been just as enthusiastic if I'd been balancing coloured balls on my nose.'

'Oh, more,' he mocked, and his eyes slid down over her with a gleam of appreciation. 'Especially if you wore a very brief costume covered in sequins.'

She had tightened at the way he looked at her and turned away. After a pause he asked, 'Why haven't you gone on to study music?'

She closed the piano with a sharp finality. 'My parents would not even hear of it.'

He had stared at her averted profile. 'I gather they're desperate to get you married off. Are you going to oblige them?'

'God knows.' Her misery had come out for a brief second in that little groan. She had laughed huskily to retrieve herself. 'They'll probably wear me down in the end. It's very hard to keep saying no to them. They are my parents.'

Her mother had come back then and given them a sharp, searching look. Drew had turned languidly, smiling with that charm of his, the grey eyes dancing. 'I'm trying to persuade your beautiful daughter to have dinner with me tomorrow.'

Helen had looked at him in surprise.

Leona had given him a peculiar, calculating stare. There was a pause, then she said sweetly, 'Of course, she'd love to.'

Drew had glanced at Helen, a taunt in his eyes. 'Good,' he had murmured, then before she could reply had drawn Leona into light chat, his black head bent her way as though she fascinated him. During the rest of the evening, Helen had seen him with other female guests and observed the same charming, intent look given to each of them. It worked like a spell. Each one seemed convinced she was fascinating him and Helen watched them light up like electric bulbs in his company.

He had barely glanced at Helen again, but that evening she had lain awake, disturbed by her memory of him. Something about him made her hair prickle on the nape of her neck. She did not trust men with charm. Too often they had learnt to use it unscrupulously.

From an early age music had been the refuge to which she fled when the world around her became intolerable. She had learnt to play at four years old purely because her grandmother had been fond of the piano and delighted by Helen's fascination with it. Grey had been ready to please his mother by engaging a teacher for Helen, but from a permissible asset her music had in time come to seem to her parents a positive menace. She wasted time at the piano which she could have spent in learning to dance, to play tennis or to flirt with the young men they knew.

Helen sighed, turning over in bed. She hoped Drew Lincoln would not want to see her again. Her parents might be furious if she froze him off as she did all other men they threw at her. They just would not take her music seriously. Hot and restless, she suddenly felt she must have a drink. As she padded across the hall, she heard her mother in the drawing-room, talking animatedly. 'No, he'll wake her up. Drew's guaranteed to get any girl he looks at, you know that. Helen will find him irresistible.'

'I don't like it,' Grey said flatly. 'I don't trust him.'

Leona laughed in tinkling amusement. 'He won't seduce her, don't be a fool. Drew wouldn't want to offend you. He'll just have some fun with her. He may break her heart a little, but that's what Helen needs—to be dragged out of her dream world. Let Drew see what he can do with her. It never lasts long with him. He tires of them.' Her voice was full of husky enjoyment and Helen shivered in protest. 'My word, he's clever at it! Plays with them like a cat with a mouse. But he gets bored once he's killed, like all cats.'

Grey broke out sharply, 'I don't want her hurt.'

'You want her married,' Leona threw back. 'The way she's going, you never will get grandchildren. Helen's frigid, in my opinion. But if anyone can break through to her, it will be Drew Lincoln.'

'And when he's moved on?' Grey asked quietly.

'She'll be easier to handle,' Leona said with a note of pure satisfaction.

Helen turned and crept back up the stairs, trembling. She had always known that her mother found her boring—Leona had made no secret of it. But to hear herself being discussed, taken apart, coldly analysed, was somehow degrading. Leona had sounded as if she enjoyed the prospect of watching her daughter being hurt by Drew Lincoln. Even her father, despite his faint protest, had not refused to allow it. The indifferent cruelty of her mother's remarks about her made Helen feel sick.

She had not cried since she was a little girl. She did not cry now. She sat on her bed, cross-legged, brushing her long hair and brooding.

Forewarned is forearmed, she told herself. Without knowing it, her mother had belled the cat. Helen would know what Drew Lincoln was up to now and she would guard against him.

Drew arrived to take her out to dinner and she met

him with a cool little smile. She had taken great care in
dressing. Her mint green dress looked mutedly alluring, the style and colour perfect. Drew's eyes drifted
over her with appreciation and when they rose to meet
her own she looked at him dispassionately, thinking:
break my heart, would he? Just let him try!

That first evening he did not even try to kiss her.
The evening was carefully controlled, Drew exerting
all his charm, his eyes smiling, teasing her a little but
gently. Helen guessed that if she had not known what
he was up to, she might have fallen for that practised
male allure. As it was, she stayed behind her bland
mask and did not show a thing.

Had he discussed her with her mother? she wondered. Presumably he had, judging by his remark to her
about her parents being desperate to get her married.
She seethed as she imagined him and Leona laughing
at her, planning her heartbreak together. The ruthless
conspiracy angered her so deeply that she wanted to hit
his smiling face, but she hid her anger and smiled back,
but always coolly, remotely.

Drew dated her frequently over the next weeks.
They danced, dined, went to the theatre, went to concerts, were seen at parties together. Helen was the
target for all his concentrated technique. Because she
was warned, she saw it in operation very clearly. Drew
knew precisely what he was doing when he lowered his
grey eyes to her face, his smile faintly crooked, his
voice husky.

The difference was, Helen also knew precisely what
he was doing. She eyed him coolly and kept him at a
distance. When he kissed her the first time, her lips
were stiff and cold under the warm brush of his mouth.

Drew made no comment. When they danced, his hand moved slowly up and down her spine, the long fingers caressing. Helen ignored it. One evening they got dragged into a car treasure hunt, sharing a back seat with two others in the noisy party. Helen found herself on Drew's lap. As they drove back in the evening his hand slid sensuously over her silken legs, his lips at her ear. She did not protest. Neither did she respond. When their eyes met, hers were blank, indifferent.

That evening Drew parked outside her home and bent to take her in his arms. There was a change in him. She felt it. His mouth bruised, demanded. His hands roved everywhere, investigating the slender shape under her sweater and skirt. She heard his heart beating under her ear, but her own stayed regular, calm. At last he drew away and looked at her levelly. 'That didn't do a thing to you, did it? Why do you see me if I leave you cold?'

'My parents insist,' she said quietly, and watched the dark red stain wash up his face.

Two days later he left England. Leona was so angry that she looked at Helen with real dislike quite openly. Helen felt triumph. She had evaded their trap. Her heart had never been touched by Drew Lincoln. The little victory bred rebellion in her. She began to defy her mother, breaking evening engagements to go to concerts, braving Leona's rage with a silent but stubborn refusal to argue.

Seated beside a thin young man in a red shirt at one concert, she found him staring at her during the music. In the interval he bought her a drink and made shy conversation about what they had been hearing. Tony Harvey was a music student living on a shoestring. He asked her to come to his college to hear a friend of his giving a recital. After the recital, Helen found herself in a noisy, excited group of young people talking about nothing but music. It was heady stuff. She walked home with Tony later, her eyes brilliant. He kissed her on the pavement outside her home and she flung her arms round him in gratitude for the pleasure of the evening, kissing him back.

As Tony bolted afterwards, flushed and elated, Helen turned to find the front door open and Drew Lincoln staring at her with a blank face.

She gave him a cool nod and walked past him. Leona and Grey gave her critical, angry looks as she went up to her room, but she no longer cared. The experience of being with people who talked her sort of language had left her walking on air.

Next day, Drew arrived at her home and found her at her piano, her face shining. Leona and Grey were both out and she looked at him uneasily as he stood in front of her.

Curtly he said, 'I've got a proposition to make to you.'

She had stared, alarmed affront creeping into her eyes. Drew's mouth twisted.

'Not that sort,' he bit out. 'I want you to marry me.'

Helen had drawn an incredulous breath, staring at him with wide dazed blue eyes. It was the last thing she had expected. She thought for a moment she was hearing things.

'First, let me explain that it wouldn't be marriage as most people understand it,' Drew had gone on hurriedly, giving her a peculiar impression that he was trying to stop her answering him. 'It would be more of a private arrangement. You see, I'd find it very useful to be your father's son-in-law—his firm is one of my biggest rivals. If I marry you, Grey will slowly let our firms merge.'

She cut in there, her voice sharp. 'Has he said so? Is this his idea?'

Drew glanced at her restlessly, his eyes not quite meeting hers. 'No,' he said flatly. 'But I'll see to it that he does agree to a merger. I'm pretty sure he'll be delighted with the idea.'

So was Helen. Her father had not believed Drew would be prepared to marry her. Drew had never been one of her father's prospects, a name on his list of possible husbands, but that been because of Drew's reputation as a bachelor, a ruthless womaniser. Given the chance, Grey would jump at him as a son-in-law. Helen knew he admired Drew, liked him. Grey would be over the moon when he knew Drew had proposed. A cold shiver ran down her back. Worse—Grey would never forgive her if she turned Drew down.

Her eyes met his and saw the knowledge of that in his narrowed stare. Drew was aware that he was going to have her parents on his side.

'My life style isn't compatible with a wife,' he said. 'I wouldn't want to drag you round the world with me. I'm always on the move, rarely anywhere for long. What I do need, though, is someone to run my homes in London, Paris and Jamaica. I use them to give my executives free holidays from the site. That would be where you came in, to keep track of the comings and goings, see the places are kept up.'

'It sounds more like a job as travelling housekeeper than a proposal of marriage,' she had said sarcastically.

'I see all the advantages to you, but what am I supposed to get out of this marvellous arrangement?'

'Freedom,' he had said. 'You don't like the way you're living at the moment. You said sooner or later your parents will force you to accept someone. Well, if you marry me, that gets them off your back, and you can lead your own life without interference.'

A little shiver ran down her spine. 'What you're suggesting is just a partnership? Not real marriage?'

He nodded. 'All you would have to do is keep up appearances. You need very rarely even see me. I'm not often in London.'

Helen had bitten her lower lip, searching for a way to ask the question she had to ask.

Drew's voice said drily beside her, 'I promise you, I shan't ask more of you than you can give, Helen. You're safe from my unwanted advances, I assure you.'

She had flushed and moved to the window to stare out, trying to make up a mental balance sheet of pros and cons. It was certainly one way out from her problems. Her parents would be ecstatic. Once married, they would leave her alone. She would be free, as Drew said.

'When I'm in London, I would like you to act as hostess to any guests I bring with me,' Drew said quietly. 'When I'm away, you can arrange your life to suit yourself, but I'm afraid I couldn't agree to having you take up music full time—that would interfere with the other duties I would need from you. You would have to be free to fly to Paris or to Jamaica. We could always arrange it so that when I'm at one, you could be at another. We need rarely meet, just often enough to make it look normal.'

Helen had stared at him. 'Would that sort of marriage work?'

He had shrugged. 'We would make it work. You wouldn't object if I led a bachelor life out of sight, would you?' The grey eyes had been level on her face. 'I like a life of variety, as you may have heard. But I shall be very discreet.'

She had hated him for saying that, but her face had been cool as she answered. 'What you did would be no concern of mine.'

She was already half convinced and Drew had known it. He had smiled in satisfaction. 'You'll be giving me what I want, Helen, and I'll make sure you get what you want, too.'

They were married two months later. Her parents were delighted, amazed. Helen wasn't involved in the complicated financial manoeuvres which had gone on, but she knew that Drew and his lawyers had come to terms with Grey. There was a condition, but of that Helen was unaware until after her wedding.

She found out on her wedding night. She had felt no tension as she undressed and slid into bed in the Jamaican villa, secure in Drew's promise that this was to be a purely platonic marriage. When he came into the room she had looked at him politely. 'Did you want something?' She had imagined he came to borrow one of the paperbacks she had brought with her on the flight, or to ask if she had an aspirin.

Instead he had given an odd, harsh crack of laughter. The sound had made her sit upright, her face paling.

He had come over to the bed and sat down on the edge of it. Helen eyed him frowningly. Drew had pushed his hands into the pockets of his short terry towelling wrap, his eyes on the frilled shade of the lamp. 'I'm sorry,' he had said. 'Your father has thrown a slight spanner into the works.'

Baffled, she had asked nervously: 'What do you mean?'

'Until you produce a grandson for him the deal's in limbo,' he had said. 'The business goes to your sons and I only get any say in things when the first one is born.'

'No!' she had exclaimed hoarsely.

Drew slowly reached out his hand and clicked off the light. Helen continued to say no at intervals, but she discovered that night that under his casual, indolent manner he had a ruthless streak.

Helen had been peculiarly innocent, unawakened to passion, untouched by desire. Drew had given her a lesson in sensuality which changed all that. He did not arouse her—she was far too angry for that. But he ripped the veil from her eyes and showed her a side of his nature which appalled her. The night was imprinted for her with sharp impressions: Drew's lips burning on her naked breasts, his hands roving silkily, exploring her shivering body without caring that she tried to thrust them away, the husky moan of his voice towards the end while she lay in shattered silence under his possessing body and hated him. By then she had given up the attempt to evade him physically, but in her mind she never surrendered.

He had slept deeply, his arm thrown over her, imprisoning her against him so that she could not escape the sound of his regular breathing, the heavy beat of his heart. Although he had been very gentle he had inevitably hurt her and she had lain awake for a long time, aching and cold.

In the morning he met her bitter stare with a twist of the mouth. 'Don't look at me like that. One son, that's all I ask.'

'You mean I have to go through that again and again until I'm pregnant?' She used a voice which was ice-cold with distaste and saw the hard flush rise in his face.

'Yes,' he had said through barely parted lips.

'I hope to God I get pregnant quickly, then,' she had said.

She had seen his eyes flash, heard the sharp intake of his breath. He had controlled his temper, though, to her regret. She had hoped to goad him into anger, but Drew, she was beginning to discover, had an enormous amount of control. That lazy, charming mask was only a mask. Underneath it lay another man, although exactly what sort of man she was not sure.

The second night he had been slightly drunk when he came to her. She suspected he had drunk to remove any inhibition her angry protests might have imposed on him. He had taken her almost without preliminaries and afterwards, although she had been silent, there were tears on her face. Drew touched them with a fingertip and said furiously, 'I hate women who cry. For God's sake ...' Breaking off, he had said curtly: 'Very well, forget it. Forget the whole damned thing.'

From the next day he had set himself to teasing her back into the relaxed frame of mind in which she had married him. He never touched her again. For the rest of their honeymoon they enjoyed the sun and sand, danced each evening, drove around and looked at the mountains and the beautiful little beaches. She found him a pleasant companion. He made her laugh.

They went back to London together, then Drew flew

off to visit one of his projects and while he was away
Helen discovered she was expecting a child. She did
not let Drew know; she did not feel she could write
the news in a letter. Drew was away for two months and
when he came back and she told him he gave her an
odd look, his brows dark.

'Will you mind?' he asked almost tentatively.

'There seems little point in minding now,' she had
said. She was having morning sickness and feeling
rotten. Her temper was brittle from lack of sleep and a
curious, drained sensation.

Drew had grimaced. 'I'm sorry.' After a hesitation,
he had asked: 'Would you like me to alter my schedule
so that I can be in London for a while?'

'Don't alter your schedule for me,' Helen had retorted.

His grey eyes had flashed. After a brief pause he had
said, 'I won't, then,' and as he said it she felt her heart
sink, as though she had missed some moment which
wouldn't come again.

He was away for most of her pregnancy. At first she
managed to leave London for Paris once or twice so that
her parents believed she was with Drew at intervals, but
as her pregnancy advanced she preferred to stay in
their London house.

Drew was in Africa when the baby was born. Helen's
father cabled him and Drew flew back at once. There
was great excitement over her production of a son. Her
father looked at her with approval for the first time in
her life, but Helen felt too tired to care. It had been a
very difficult birth; her body was too slender, her hips
too narrow, for it to be easy.

Drew stood at her bedside and looked at her guardedly. 'He's very beautiful,' he said. 'Thank you. Had you thought of a name?'

'He's your son,' she had said bitterly. 'You think of one.'

His lips had tightened. 'Stephen,' he said curtly.

She had closed her eyes. 'Very well.'

All the time she was wondering what was making her talk to him like this and getting no answer. She knew he was standing there staring at her. She was very pale, her skin waxen, her pale hair emphasising the weary look of her features. Depression hung over her like fog. She felt like crying all the time and did not know why.

A nurse came in and said coyly that it was really time that Mr Lincoln kissed his wife goodbye.

Helen opened her eyes and saw his dark face stoop towards her. He kissed her lightly on the lips. 'Get some sleep,' he had said.

When she left the hospital with the baby, Drew had a nanny waiting to take over the care. Helen had not even thought of hiring one; she had wanted to look after the baby herself. During the fortnight in the hospital she had found it heavenly to hold the soft warm little body in her arms and look at Stephen's blank blue stare as it tried to focus on her face.

Pride would not let her argue with Drew, though. He had made his decision and she let it rest. She was breast-feeding the baby, so she spent a good deal of her time with him, and as Drew was overseas again she found her life revolving around her son.

When Drew came back to London she and Stephen had just left for a month in Jamaica. Drew did not

follow them. She returned when he left for an Arab
state and when he came back from there, she and
Stephen were in Paris.

For the next two years they almost never met, but
Drew did come out to Jamaica during one of their
visits and spend some days with them.

'I'm sure you'll forgive me if I spend a little time
with my son,' he had drawled.

She had not replied, looking away. Under the eyes of
the servants they were smilingly polite to each other
and the mask they were forced to assume in public became slowly the mask they wore in private.

Drew lapsed into teasing now and then, his eyes
mocking her, and she grew used to responding in kind.
Their relationship smoothed out into a strange sort of
distant intimacy. Drew sometimes rang from abroad if
he knew that Stephen had a cold or was teething painfully. Stephen was their bridge. They met on terms of
guarded friendship over their son. If she cared to read
gossip columns she could occasionally pick up clues as
to his current mistress. Drew was never obvious about
it, but once or twice she caught sight of him with some
woman and she knew there was always someone in his
life. He had warned her about that and she accepted it.

Her own life was very busy. Apart from the running
of their various homes, she liked to spend a good deal of
time with Stephen. As he got older their days fell into
a quiet pattern. Helen took him for a walk each day
with their dachshund, Max, whose eel-like body could
wriggle into impossible places. Stephen adored him,
often chasing after him into shrubberies in the park
from which they both emerged grubby and panting.

Helen also had her own friends, one of whom had

once been her father's secretary. Janet had had to leave the job when she became pregnant. Her husband was an engineer with the firm, and, like Drew, often abroad. Janet had gone with him once, but unfortunately she had found that hot countries made her very ill. She had a skin allergy which broke out in heat. After her baby was born she was restless, bored with her small London flat, wanting some other occupation, yet not wishing to leave the baby. She began to do typing at home. When the baby was three she had found a place in a day nursery for it and started work again, but found it too difficult to cope with a baby and a full-time job. Talking to Helen about it, Helen had suggested looking for part-time work and Janet had groaned. 'Along with everybody else! It's very hard to get.'

Helen had had a brainwave. Together she and Janet had started a secretarial agency specialising in part-time work. Helen put up the capital and Janet did most of the work. It had grown rapidly and now had a very good turn-over. More importantly, it gave both of them a sense of purpose. They had great fun running the agency. Helen took over one day a week so that Janet could spend time with her child.

The years of marriage had settled into a set pattern which she had begun to think of as fixed, immutable. But now, aware of Drew beside her, his long legs casually thrust out across the car, she felt oddly as if that pattern were shifting suddenly. Drew had acted out of character, breaking his habits, by coming to Paris without warning. It was something he had never done before—going anywhere without giving her warning. Her frown deepened. Was it sheer chance that he was here or had he come deliberately?

Their apartment block stood in a quiet Paris street which only came to life during the morning and evening rush hours when traffic flowed through it for a short period as people made their way into the heart of the city and then came home again.

When they arrived, Drew walked round and helped her from the car, his hand under her elbow, every inch the solicitous husband, then dealt with the driver before ushering her into the cool foyer of the block. The concierge peered at them as they walked towards the lift. She and her husband lived in a small flat on the premises, supervising the maintenance of the stairs and corridors, manning the telephone switch board, keeping an eagle eye on who came in and who went out, and when.

The housekeeper who ran their apartment had a long-running feud with the concierge, with which she always insisted on burdening Helen, giving her chapter and verse for the various insults they flung at each other as Madame Lefeuvre went to and fro under the eye of the concierge.

The lift moved purringly upwards. Drew lounged beside Helen, his eyes on her profile. She was only now beginning to realise that they would be alone that evening, and to be concerned about that.

Madame Lefeuvre opened the door of the apartment and her look of disbelief made Helen tense. '*Madame, monsieur*, we had not expected you both! There must have been some mistake. Ah, what a surprise. I shall have to make up Monsieur's room.' And then, quite distinctly, Helen caught a sly look cross her dark face, saw her look glintingly at Drew, a silent question mark in her face.

Helen flushed. 'How are you, *madame*? Very well, I hope.'

'Very well,' Madame Lefeuvre replied. Although Helen spoke French it was a trifle limpingly and she preferred to stick to her own tongue because she felt uneasy in any other.

Drew, on the other hand, spoke French like a native and at once greeted Madame Lefeuvre, '*Tout va bien, eh?*'

Helen walked past them into the long, green marble-floored hall, with its trailing ferns in white porcelain bowls and white velvet-upholstered seats. Drew had given her a free hand with the decor in all his homes, brushing aside questions of expense, and she had created an elegant setting in this apartment, one which she now viewed with pleasure.

Drew and Madame Lefeuvre talked in their rapid, gunfire French behind her, laughing.

Crossing into the salon, Helen sighed with grateful relief. Cool, shadowy, the white blinds drawn and the walls criss-crossed with soft lines of sunshine, it seemed to welcome her. Although her home in London was her main home, this Paris apartment was the place she loved most. She threw herself down on to the straw-coloured couch, piling motley satin cushions behind her head, their colours jewelled and gleaming, blue, pink and yellow.

What, she asked herself, was she going to do? She had never spent any time alone with Drew since their honeymoon. How long did he mean to stay in Paris? What were his plans?

He stood nearby, his hands in his pockets in a typical stance, the jacket of his casual suit open, his shirt unbuttoned part way down, his black head cocked. 'Why didn't you bring Stephen?' he asked oddly.

Helen looked at him as if in surprise at his presence. Coolly, she shrugged. 'His best friend Angus has a birthday party tomorrow and I knew Stephen would hate to miss it. I shall only be here for a few days.'

The door opened and Madame Lefeuvre came into the room carrying a tray. She placed it on a rich rosewood table near the couch. 'Shall I pour the coffee, *madame*?'

Helen swung her long legs to the floor. 'No, thank you. I'll do it.'

When the woman had gone, giving them both a curious look, Helen poured the strong black coffee, glanced at Drew and asked: 'Are you taking sugar?'

'No,' he said. 'Just cream.'

She added a swirl of cream and he wandered over to the couch and sat down beside her. His proximity bothered Helen. It always did. She tried to draw unobtrusively away and Drew gave her the derisive look he always gave when he noticed her attempts to keep him at a distance.

'How long are you staying?' she asked.

He sipped his coffee, his wide shoulders lifting in a slight shrug. 'A few days.'

There was a little silence. Drew looked into his coffee. 'Tell me, are there any men in your life?'

Helen felt heat in her throat. Swallowing, she gave him a cold look. 'What has that to do with you? I don't ask you questions about your private life.'

'Ask away,' he drawled, his eyes insolent again.

'I have no interest in it,' she retorted.

His smile was cold. 'Ah, but I have an interest in yours.'

'What right do you have to take one?' she asked furiously, her face flushing.

'I know Stephen's mine. I want to be as sure about any other children you might produce.'

'Oh!' she exclaimed, stiffening, reddening, her eyes staring at him in rage. 'How dare you? And anyway, we've gone our own way for years. Why the sudden interest in how I spend my time?'

He lowered thick black lashes. 'While I was talking to Stephen the other day he mentioned an Uncle James.'

'James Farrier,' she said tartly. 'I've told you about him. He's the accountant who's looking after the agency accounts.'

'Married?'

'No,' she said defiantly.

Drew's lashes lifted and the grey eyes were hard. 'Don't get ideas, will you, Helen?'

She stared at him. 'What's that supposed to mean?'

'Women will allow emotion to cloud an issue,' he drawled. 'Our arrangement has worked beautifully. Let's keep it that way, shall we? I don't want you jeopardising everything by falling for someone and running off with him. Your father might get difficult.'

Helen poured herself some more coffee to give herself time to cool down. When she had added cream to it she took a sip, lowered the cup again and said coldly: 'You have no need to worry. I have no intention of doing anything of the kind. Our arrangement works as well for me as it does for you. I've no wish to change it.'

'Cold-blooded little bitch, aren't you?' Drew got up and strolled to the door. Over his shoulder he said softly, 'I'm in for dinner, by the way. I have no appointments tonight. I've told Madame Lefeuvre that Philip will arrive tomorrow and she's getting his room ready.'

When he had gone she could have kicked herself for not having invented a dinner date. She looked at the white telephone, biting her lip. She knew a number of people in Paris, but one could hardly telephone and ask to be invited to dinner.

She was not looking forward to dining alone with Drew, however. The more she saw of him the more dangerous it became. She could only maintain the smooth façade of her manner to him if she kept him at a distance. Any time spent with him caused tiny cracks in that façade. Although he had not laid a hand on her since their honeymoon she was not unaware of the fact that if she showed him the slightest encouragement, Drew would willingly make love to her. He was a man who enjoyed sensuality; she knew him enough to know that. Occasionally he had shown her a brief glimpse of it. His eyes held caressing interest when he looked at her in some moods. He would not be slow to respond if she gave him a green light, but Helen had no intention of ever doing so. She did not want that sort of relationship with him. She would find it humiliating and degrading to become one of Drew's women, an occasional amusement for him when he chose to visit her bed.

From time to time at parties in London, during his infrequent appearances, she had seen him with women and although nothing ever showed on the surface, she had developed antennae which warned her when Drew had had affairs with people. There was something in the way they looked at each other, a warm comprehension, a teasing intimacy. Their voices would have a certain tone, their smiles would be familiar.

She did not like it. It wasn't that she was jealous, she hurriedly told herself. She didn't care a straw what he did. But she did not care to be aware of it, to have it forced to her attention.

Thumping one of the satin cushions, she lay down on the couch again, her feet crossed, her body relaxed. She would have to play it cool, that was all. She could do that, for heaven's sake, she had had enough practice.

Philip Cameron was one of Drew's engineers. She had met him once before. He had come to London for two days from Africa, a tall bronzed man with a deep-toned voice and a quiet smile. She had been touched when he brought Stephen a wooden puppet of a giraffe made in Kenya. When one pulled the tail the neck waved to and fro and the long legs clicked. Stephen had been enchanted with it. It had been a thoughtful gesture on the part of a man who had not even got any children. Philip was married, she remembered, but childless, something he regretted.

His presence at the apartment would certainly relieve the nervous strain of Drew's company. He would be here tomorrow, she gathered, so she only had to get through this one evening.

It might be a peculiar arrangement they had, but it was one that had worked so far and she did not want anything to disturb the balance between them.

Frowning, she recalled his remarks about James. Odd that Stephen should have mentioned James. For some reason, the little boy did not like him. Every time James came to the house, Stephen scowled at him and on one terrible occasion he had actually bitten his hand. James had been talking to Helen about something to do with the agency, and Stephen had climbed on to her lap, interposing himself between them. James had given him a rather stiff smile and said lightly: 'You're too big to sit on Mummy's lap now, Stephen my lad. Off you go.' He had moved to dislodge Stephen quite gently and Stephen with a little growl had bitten his hand.

Helen had been horrified. Stephen had been dismissed to his room and it had taken her an hour to smooth James down. If Stephen had been a dog, she had realised, James would have been convinced he had rabies.

He was a very conventional man, polite, well-mannered, helpful. She could never fathom what made Stephen detest him, but the boy made no attempt to hide his furious reaction whenever he saw James.

What, she wondered, had he said to his father on the telephone? A flush ran up her cheeks. Drew had never shown signs of suspecting her of having any entanglements with men before. Why had he done so now? What on earth could Stephen have said to him?

She watched the dying of the afternoon sunshine. Reluctantly she got up and went into her own bedroom to shower and change into something more formal for dinner. Emerging from the cubicle later with an enormous fluffy pink towel wrapped around her body, she halted in shocked surprise to find Drew in her bedroom, his shirt hanging open, fiddling with his cuffs.

'I can't fix this,' he said casually. 'Have a go, will you?'

Barefooted she padded over the deep rose carpet. He

raised his dark head to give her a swift all-over glance.
She met his eyes coldly.

'Let me see,' she bit out.

He extended his wrist and Helen bent over the cuff-
link. The clasp was stiff and would not give. After a
moment of struggle she felt it click.

'There,' she said, raising her head.

'Your towel's slipping,' Drew said silkily. Before she
could stop him he had slid his hand inside the towel,
between her breasts, and softly tugged it upward.
'There,' he said with a taunting little smile, then he
turned and strolled out.

As the door closed she glared at it helplessly. She
could still feel the cool brush of his fingers on her skin.
Drew was going to be difficult, she thought. He was at
a loose end and he was looking for amusement. Well, he
wasn't getting any from her!

CHAPTER TWO

HELEN had learned to dress for effect, knowing precisely what sort of impression she should make on whatever audience she would be facing. In his infrequent visits to London Drew had occasionally given her advice on her clothes and he had always been amazingly clever about it. Years of experience with women, she thought cynically. He was a man with a clear, retentive brain. Give him five minutes and he could pick up a smattering of any language or any subject. Helen had heard him speak African dialects, Arabic, most European languages, and even launch into broad Yorkshire. His ear picked up intonation like a Geiger counter. If he turned his attention to anything he mastered it. So she had taken seriously what he said about clothes and bought her wardrobe with his instructions in mind.

Tonight she stood in front of her enormous wardrobe, viewing her dresses doubtfully, looking for one which was elegant without being alluring. She wanted to keep him at a safe distance without being too obvious about it.

Taking down a high-necked, long-sleeved dress in a smoky grey chiffon she held it against herself and decided it would do. Later, staring at her own reflection, she wasn't quite so sure. True, it covered most of her body from her neck to her calves, but although it was so discreet there was something indefinably challenging about it. She bit her lip, then shrugged. Too late to change her mind.

Drew stood with a glass of whisky in his hand, staring at the soft, faded colours of the tapestry. Standing in the doorway, Helen viewed him with reluctance, angrily forced to admit that lazy attraction of his, wondering how he managed to fasten his mask of good humour over the ruthless iron of his real nature and convince so many people that the man they saw in a social setting was the whole man. She knew different, yet even she had no real idea about what happened inside that head of his, and she wondered if she ever would.

He turned his dark head with a characteristic motion and she caught the upwards flick of his brows as he took in her dress. Sardonic amusement glimmered in his eyes. 'Very elegant,' he said smoothly, and she knew that he was perfectly aware of her reasons for wearing such a discreet dress. 'What will you drink?' he continued, however, without further comment.

'Sherry,' she said, moving to the couch. 'Dry, please.'

He walked to the decanters and she found herself watching the casual grace of his movements. As he turned, the glass of pale liquid in his hand, she hurriedly switched her gaze to the tapestry. He came over to her and she took the glass, her fingers careful not to touch his, her eyes not reaching his face but aware, all the same, of his mocking smile as he noted her avoidance of his touch.

He sat down beside her, turning towards her, one long leg crossed over the other, his arm snaking along the back of the couch, his other hand holding his own drink.

She sipped her sherry, head bent. She knew he was looking at her, his eyes slowly wandering from the thin chiffon covering her throat and shoulders to the full folds of the skirt. Her skin glowed through the pale material with a soft, pearly gleam, her hair glinted under the light, the fine silken strands pulled tightly back from her face.

'Tell me, Helen,' he asked suddenly, 'has there been anyone in the past five years?'

She felt her glass quiver in her fingers. A rush of pink stained her cheeks. 'If there had been, I wouldn't tell you,' she retorted angrily.

'I thought not,' he observed with an unhidden satisfaction. 'If anything of the kind ever happened to you it would show.'

'Such experience,' she mocked, her eyes flaring.

He grinned. 'You disapprove of me, don't you, Helen?'

'I never think about you,' she threw back.

The grey eyes narrowed, losing their smile. 'Don't tempt me to make you,' he said forcefully.

She drew back from the hard stare, alarm in her blue eyes. 'I don't want to tempt you to do anything. You said yourself, we have a perfect arrangement, one that suits us both. Let's keep it that way.'

'You bloodless little virgin,' he muttered, lifting his glass to his mouth, his head averted from her.

'Virgin?' she queried sarcastically.

Drew turned then and gave her a savage smile. 'Oh, yes, despite the son you've given me, that's what you are. Virgin territory, untouched, stony. I sometimes wonder if you're human at all. Physically you've matured into a beautiful woman, mentally you're a frozen mystery.'

'There's nothing mysterious about me,' she said,

thinking that all the mystery was on his side. After six years she knew no more about him than she had the day she married him.

Twirling the glass between his long hands he stared into the amber liquid, watching the light sparkle on the crystal facets as though it fascinated him. 'Your parents have never taken any interest in you, have they? I've listened to those polite little chats you have with them and thought you might all be total strangers to each other.'

'We have little in common,' she agreed.

'Your father's obsession about heirs can explain his attitude, but what about your mother?'

'Leona?' She laughed coolly, shrugging.

'She's too busy being fascinating to have time to give a damn for anyone else?' Drew suggested.

Helen did not dispute it or confirm it. 'She leads her own life,' she replied without inflection.

'You're very tolerant,' he said with a bite. 'You let us all do that, don't you? Your parents, me—you don't ask or want anything from us, and you expect us to accord you the same favour.'

He sounded as though he were making an accusation, and Helen resented it. Stiffly she said: 'Isn't that what you wanted? After all, you suggested our arrangement. It was your idea.'

His mouth twisted. He lowered his eyes to the tips of his black shoes. 'True. And you jumped at it. It took you out of an intolerable situation. At the time, I got the idea you were becoming desperate.'

Looking back, she realised that she had, Drew was quite right. Her aimless, boring social life had been driving her insane. If she had not married him and escaped, she would either have run away and perhaps got herself into an even worse situation, or married someone out of sheer desperation. Frowning, she glanced at him and found him watching her with speculative eyes.

'Who was the fellow you were kissing the night before I asked you to marry me?' he asked abruptly, taking her by surprise.

Her eyes widened. 'I'd forgotten him.' A faint amusement came into her face. 'He was a music student. We met by accident. I barely knew him.'

'You didn't see him again, then?'

She shook her head. Tony had rung her, but she had not dared to see him again. Her parents had been so angry with her about the little incident and after Drew's proposal somehow she had been reluctant to rebel again. Accepting him had delighted her parents so much that for a time things had been smooth at home.

'Have you ever cared for anything or anyone, Helen?' Drew asked with a strange intonation.

'Stephen,' she said at once.

His face changed and he looked at her wryly. 'Of course. Well, for Stephen, at least, we must be thankful.'

'I am,' she said, smiling.

His eyes dropped to the warm curve of her mouth. 'You should do that more often. It suits you.'

A faint pink ran under her skin. She hated it when he paid her compliments. She could not forget how often he must have paid them to other women and how insincerely they must be meant. He watched her eyes darken, and a dry irony crept into his face.

'Aren't I even allowed to notice that when you smile you look twice as beautiful?'

'I dislike flattery,' she flung at him.

'That wasn't flattery,' he said, his mouth hardening. 'Don't you know the truth when you see it?'

'I didn't think you would.'

'My God! Your opinion of me is around zero, isn't it?' He got up and went over to the decanter to refill his glass and she could not stop herself from watching the movements of the long, lithe body. In his formal black evening dress he had a dangerous attraction, the cut of the clothes designed to emphasise the athletic fitness of the strong body beneath them: the broad shoulders, deep chest and that tapering slimness from waist to thigh. He walked with the supple, predatory stalk of an animal, a leisured menace about his stride, as though at any moment he might shed that lazy air and strike.

The black hair was thick and full, brushed back from his face in a casual fashion, the ends of it tapering into his collar. Watching the way it picked up the light, Helen suddenly had a flashing image of herself on the night they were married, trying to stop him by yanking at that hair and merely making him laugh softly, as though the feel of her fingers in it pleased him.

Drew turned and she flushed deeply. His eyes narrowed on her. She looked away, angry with herself, knowing that every tiny hint of self-betrayal was picked up by that cold brain of his and shrewdly interpreted.

'Another sherry?' he asked.

She shook her head, indicating silently that she had not finished the one in her hand. Drew came back towards her and sat down. She noted with a fresh quiver of alarm that he was closer, his thigh resting against the fullness of her skirt. She would have liked to move away, but something in the way he was watching her made her sit very still.

'Why is Philip coming to Paris?' she asked in the hope of changing the far too intimate nature of their conversation.

His mouth was crooked as he glanced at her and his eyes indicated that he knew her motive in asking the question. However, he answered coolly. 'I thought he needed the break.'

'Is he ill?' She frowned, sorry to hear that. She had liked Philip very much when they met.

'Tired,' Drew shrugged.

'Is his wife coming with him?'

Giving her a sharp look, Drew shook his head. 'She's dead. Didn't I tell you?'

'Dead?' Helen was shocked. 'No! But when? How? What happened?'

'She drowned,' Drew said curtly. 'Her boat over- turned while she was sailing on Lake Kowoli. They think she may have disturbed some hippo—they're a hazard out there. Normally they won't interfere with anyone, but sometimes if there are young with them, the parents get nasty. God knows what happened, but her boat was overturned and by the time anyone could get there, she'd gone.'

'How dreadful! When was this?'

'Three months ago.'

'I wish you'd told me,' she said, frowning. 'I would have liked to write to Philip and give him my con- dolences.'

Drew threw her a quick look. 'I saw to all that. He was in quite a state afterwards, but he refused to take time off. Said he needed to work and at the time I thought it might help. Lately he's been looking like grey string, though. I told him to come to Paris for a conference on some new machinery. There's a factory a few miles from Paris making some equipment we could find very useful. I guessed he wouldn't agree to a holiday, but his sense of duty made him agree to leave the site to come and see these machines.'

Helen sighed. 'Poor Philip! It must have been a terrible blow for him. They'd been married for some time, hadn't they?'

'Yes,' said Drew, his face dry. 'And their marriage was about as real as ours.'

She turned a shocked face to him. 'What?'

He smiled tightly. 'She was a promiscuous little bitch—led Philip a rotten life. He's well rid of her, but he hadn't expected that to happen. Half his grief is due to a feeling of guilt. He was planning to divorce her and now he's torturing himself by believing he willed what happened.'

'But how terrible,' she said, remembering Philip's sensitive, intelligent eyes and believing that he would react like that.

'Philip has an oversized conscience,' Drew muttered. 'I'd like to bang his head on a wall. It wasn't his fault that the stupid woman got herself killed, but he's going through hell believing it.'

'Conscience wouldn't mean much to you, would it?' she asked with a trace of bitterness.

He turned his head and looked at her coldly. 'That's

a pretty sweeping statement. I take responsibility for
my own actions but never for anyone else's—life is too
short.'

'And yours is too hectic,' she agreed. 'Did you, by
any chance, happen to be one of his wife's lovers?'

She saw the icy flare of the grey eyes. 'No, I was not,'
he bit out. 'I have a rule never to get involved with the
wives of any of my men. Do you think I want that sort
of trouble? There are enough tensions on site without
adding sexual jealousy to them.'

Helen looked away, her fingers trembling on the
stem of her glass. Drew's anger sounded in his voice.

After a moment he said with a sneer, 'Don't apologise, will you?'

'I'm sorry,' she said hurriedly. 'If I jumped to conclusions it's only because you yourself told me that
you went in for that sort of brief affair.'

'Not on the site,' he said harshly. 'In general I don't
encourage my men to have their wives around at all. It
just slows work up and complicates the problems. Some
of them insist on having their families nearby, though,
and I can hardly stop them.'

'But you set them a good example by keeping yours
safely in London,' she said sarcastically.

'I was frank with you when I asked you to marry me.
Ours was a marriage of convenience—on both sides.'

Aware that he was staring at her, she nodded, her
eyes lowered, her cheeks flushed.

Madame Lefeuvre suddenly opened the door and
beamed upon them. 'Dinner is ready,' she said coyly.
'If Madame and Monsieur please.'

Helen got up and put down her unfinished sherry,
conscious of Drew's sardonic, pointed smile. He was as

aware as she was that the housekeeper's excitement had its roots in a belief that they were here together for romantic reasons, and Drew was amused by it.

Walking into the dining-room, she allowed Drew to pull back her chair. As she sat down, he bent forward and she felt his lips deliberately tingling across her white nape just below the coil of her hair.

Madame Lefeuvre positively palpitated—Helen heard her little sigh of enjoyment. Drew sat down across the table and his grey glance mocked Helen silently. She gave him a brief glare of dislike.

He had always taken advantage of any opening fate threw him. Drew was too acquisitive. She had seen it for a long time in his business dealings, picking up hints of his deals from her father's admiring, gleeful gossip about him. Drew took whatever opportunities he could, whether it was of profit for his firm, or profit for himself as far as women were concerned.

Helen's blue eyes were chilly as she unfolded her napkin and laid it across her knees. She was not letting him take anything from her.

Madame Lefeuvre served their meal discreetly, sliding out of the room with another coy smile, leaving them alone.

'I wish you'd keep your hands to yourself!' Helen snapped as soon as Madame had gone.

'I know you do,' Drew drawled, his eyes on his melon.

'Then why do you do it?'

As soon as she had asked that she knew it had been a stupid question, and Drew's shout of amusement underlined that. His eyes teased her across the table, he gave her a mock leer.

'Need you ask?' He dropped his glance appreciatively over her and she was tempted to pick up her plate and chuck it at him. Controlling the impulse she gave a faint sigh of baffled rage. There was no point in argument with Drew. He always won and her annoyance only gave him further amusement.

Eyes on the pale green flesh of the melon, she thought of the rest of the evening with dismay. She did not know how she was going to get through it under those mocking, cynical eyes. He saw too much, knew too much, a sophisticated, experienced man who enjoyed teasing her because her innocence was in such contrast to his own knowledge. He had a hard, clever mind and a body which had an alarming, potent sexuality. He had never needed to exert himself—life had handed him everything on a plate. Lazily smiling, he sauntered through life with the enjoyment of someone who knows he only has to stretch out a hand to get what he wants.

Madame Lefeuvre came in to remove their plates and serve a delicately flavoured veal in a sauce made with peppers and celery. Drew's black lashes drooped as Madame slid softly around behind Helen. He leant over the table and, before Helen could move her hand, had lifted it to his lips, his mouth brushing her knuckles. 'A pity Philip is arriving tomorrow. It will break into our delightful idyll.'

Taking a leaf from his book, Helen made no effort to regain her hand. She deliberately gave him a sweet smile. 'Ah, but I do enjoy Philip's company,' she said. 'He's very attractive.'

She felt Drew's hand tighten on hers. Madame gave her a shocked, reproachful look before she went out.

Drew stared across the table, his eyes speculative. Helen snatched her hand back and picked up her fork.

'You're playing a dangerous game,' Drew observed thoughtfully. 'It's rare for you to try a reprisal. Interesting.'

'Just stop trying to make a fool of me!' she bit back, her blue eyes chilly. 'Just because Madame is being absurd there's no reason why we should follow suit.'

Bending her head she began to eat and after a few seconds, Drew also turned to his plate. The food easily surpassed that of their London housekeeper, the rice full and fluffy, the veal perfectly cooked and very tender. While she ate, Helen wondered how she could without being too obvious escape from this dangerous intimacy with him.

'*Do* you think Philip is attractive?' Drew asked idly, and she looked up in surprise.

'Yes,' she said coolly.

He pushed his plate away and leaned back in his chair, the black jacket open, revealing the strong, muscular contours of his chest. 'So Philip is your idea of the ideal man?'

She caught the note of derision and gave him a dry smile. 'I didn't say that, but no one could deny he was attractive—very kind and friendly, the sort of man most people like.'

'And at the moment in need of distraction,' Drew added.

She stiffened. 'In that case, my presence would only inhibit you. I suggest I go to a hotel tomorrow.'

His glance was wickedly amused. 'My God, what sort of orgies are you anticipating?'

She threw him a furious look. 'You've never made

any secret of your liking for feminine company in your leisure hours.'

'How right you are,' he drawled. 'But do you really see Philip joining in with any degree of enthusiasm?'

'No,' she accepted. 'No, I imagine Philip wouldn't have much taste for that sort of thing.'

'But I would?'

She met his eyes and found them icy. 'So you've given me to understand.'

'When have I ever implied that my taste ran to orgies?' he asked sarcastically. 'Personally, I prefer my women one at a time.'

Helen shrugged. 'Whatever.'

'I like women,' he went on tersely, his anger growing at her tone, 'but that doesn't mean I spend every leisure moment leaping from bed to bed. Most men do like women, you know, and vice versa. You're the exception, Helen, not me. Your dislike of the male sex amounts to a phobia.'

'Just because I didn't fall on my face for you it doesn't mean I dislike men in general,' she said sharply.

'Have you ever been so much as interested in one?' he enquired with a sardonic smile.

'That's my business.'

'Mine too, I fancy, since you're my wife.'

'You're my husband, but I'm not interested in what you get up to,' she retorted.

He drew a short, sharp breath and put his hands on the table, his palms flat, leaning towards her. 'Sometimes I could hit you,' he gritted through barely parted lips, his voice biting. 'When we married it was not a normal arrangement, so I saw no need to curtail my leisure activities.'

'Did I ever ask you to?'

'Oh, no,' he said, smiling coldly. 'You preferred things the way they were. Our set up suited you as much as it suited me. We were neither of us ready for a real marriage then.'

'We aren't now,' she said.

'How right you are,' Drew muttered, drawing back.

Helen sat up stiffly as Madame Lefeuvre swam softly back into the room, her eager black glance roving from one to the other of them, scenting the faint tension in the atmosphere and clearly misreading it. They both refused either the chocolate soufflé she offered or the cheese board. With a disappointed moue of regret she suggested that they take their coffee into the salon.

The wine they had drunk with the dinner left a faint cloudy dullness on Helen's mind. She sank on to the couch and viewed Drew's back with regret. 'Brandy?' he asked, turning as he poured a glass for himself.

'No, thank you,' she said at once. She knew she had drunk enough wine to loosen her inhibitions. Any more could be dangerous. She was already finding herself saying things she would not normally have said. Her unusual sharpness over dinner had been caused, she saw now, by the effect of the wine she had been drinking.

'Nonsense,' said Drew, coming back with two glasses. 'A touch of brandy will help you sleep.'

Madame came in with the coffee as she was shaking her head and Drew firmly put the glass into her hand, tilting his own. 'Cheers,' he said softly.

'Bonne nuit, madame, monsieur,' breathed Madame Lefeuvre as she backed from the room.

Helen looked at the brandy in her full-bowled glass and with a faint shiver of recklessness began to drink it.

The heat ran through her body wildly and she felt colour draining into her face.

Drew sat down beside her and again she felt his long, muscular thigh touching her own. She looked at him through her lashes, heat in her veins. He leaned over and took her glass. The brandy had gone—she was surprised to realise that. She had not realised how quickly she was drinking it.

Drew turned towards her, his lean body lounging casually against the back of the couch.

Alarmed, she said huskily, 'Would you like me to play for you?'

He caught her arm as she half rose. 'Not yet,' he said softly. 'Tell me, how are your lessons coming?'

'Very well,' she answered. Glancing at the coffee pot she said, 'I'll pour the coffee, then, shall I?'

His mouth twisted. 'Of course,' he said, and released her. She poured the coffee with hands that shook slightly, and knew that as she did so he watched her intently, his eyes gleaming like dark water through those long thick lashes. How unfair of fate to give lashes like that to a man, she thought idly. They enhanced those clever grey eyes far too much, and Drew used them wickedly, as he was using them now, aware of the effect he could have with them.

Helen handed him his cup and sat back to sip her own coffee. She did so far too quickly. It was hot and she almost gasped at the heat on her tongue, but it gave her something to do and kept them occupied quite safely. She was beginning to feel more and more nervous; more and more aware of him.

'Do you realise how rarely we've ever been alone?' Drew asked her coolly.

Realise it? The realisation was driving her out of her mind, she thought. She was beginning to have dangerous, insane impulses flashing around her brain and it was a struggle to force them down out of sight.

'Six years of marriage and a son, yet we know as little about each other now as we did the day we married,' he went on quietly.

'That was the arrangement,' she shrugged.

'And you never regret having made it?' he asked, watching her without expression.

She couldn't meet his eyes. What was he trying to do? Make her admit what? Helen refused to look up, refused to answer.

He moved and she started, her head going up with a faint stifled gasp. Removing her empty cup he gave her a sardonic look. 'Do you know what you're doing?' he asked her drily. 'Do you realise how much of life you're wasting? Come out from behind that wall of yours, Helen. Doesn't it ever get claustrophobic in there?'

The lazy amusement had evaporated as though it had never existed, as though the hard, sensual face had never worn any look but the one it wore now, the grey eyes glittering between their long lashes, the skin stretched tautly over his bones. She felt her own body clench in sudden, incredible tension. His eyes wandered over her in a cool, leisurely examination and then came back to her face, her throat closed in shock as she saw what lay in them.

He leant towards her and her nostrils filled with the astringent scent of his body.

'No,' she almost whimpered, shrinking back. 'If you lay one finger on me I'll scream!'

He slowly extended one finger and touched her between the breasts deliberately, staring into her eyes.

Helen drew a deep gasping breath. The finger stroked sensually along the deep valley between her breasts, burning through the thin chiffon and leaving a trail of heat over her skin.

'Don't,' she whispered shakily, but when he bent his black head she didn't move away. His lips closed over her own fiercely, in such a deep and savage kiss that she felt her mouth filling with the taste of him, her body stiffening in shock. She put up her hands to his broad shoulders to push him away, but she couldn't move him. He was pushing her down among the cushions, his hands slipping down over her to cup her breasts, fondling the round smooth flesh beneath the chiffon with such slow sensuality that Helen abruptly closed her eyes and felt herself slacken in weak surrender.

Drew lifted his head at last and she opened her dazed eyes to look at him incredulously. The hot glitter in his glance made her heart miss a beat.

'It could be very good for us,' he whispered thickly. 'You're wasting that sweetness, Helen. What use will your long-preserved virginity be to you in the grave?'

She felt a wild increase of panic. Drew was pressing her too close. She knew the temptation he was offering her, she knew too well that it was nagging away at her to accept what he was offering. She thrust his hands away and struggled up.

'No!' she said, and fled from the room in trembling disarray.

CHAPTER THREE

IN her own room, she regretted for the first time that she could not make herself give way to the desire filling her. She had evaded Drew for years without too much regret, but then Drew had never come so close before. Even on the two nights he had made love to her on their honeymoon he had been using more force than persuasion, and, she suspected, he had done so because he had been aware that she would never have given in to persuasion. At that time she had been hostile, resistant. Any advances from Drew would undoubtedly have been met with cold distaste.

From the salon she heard the muted whisper of music and knew that Drew was neither following her nor going to bed. Sighing, she herself went into the bathroom and took a shower. The warm water slightly relieved the pressure caused by too much wine. She felt less cloudy in her mind.

She read for a while, then turned out the light and lay in the dark listening to the distant music.

She had locked her door but, nevertheless, she listened with faint anxiety as she heard him moving outside. He walked past without pausing. Helen sagged on her pillows. A peculiar mixture of relief and regret seeped into her. She had half wanted him to stop and try her door. He hadn't, which must mean that his advances had been half-hearted, and that stung.

If she had given herself to him it would have meant

nothing to him but yet another coolly deliberate conquest. He was a sensualist who liked variety, who enjoyed the chase more than the kill, who tired rapidly of his victims. A cat, she thought, a cruel, ruthless, soft-padding animal who enjoyed playing with his prey before he took it. He had been playing with her all evening. She had been aware of it, angry about it, helpless to do anything to stop him. She had known the danger from the moment she saw him at the airport. Alarm had sprung to life inside her from the moment she set eyes on him.

She felt her face burning and put her hands over it. Why had she been so afraid of being alone with him? Even as she asked herself the question she knew the answer. Deep inside herself she had known for a long time.

She had found Drew attractive from their first meeting, but her mother's amused remarks about him breaking her heart had ended that attraction—she had imagined, for ever, but angrily she had to recognise that it had outlasted her own fury over Leona's conspiracy with him. She had resisted his attraction, but she had been aware of it. She had never been in love, never remotely felt she could be in love. What she felt towards Drew was a physical chemistry which had nothing to do with the emotions.

It was powerful, for all that. It was fomenting inside her now, demanding satisfaction. It had to be stifled, smothered, forced down.

Her feelings towards her son were safe feelings. Stephen needed her, loved her, and Helen needed and loved him. They were equal in their response. Every other human being bore the seeds of misery, though.

And especially Drew—that sophisticated, cynical face of his told its own story. He was a man who could only hurt her. When he kissed her tonight he had given her exquisite pleasure, and she had wanted more. Yet now she was aching, and if it happened again, the pain would be worse. She could become weakly addicted to him, unable to live without him, and Helen would not permit herself such a piece of folly.

The bored indifference of her parents had taught her at an early age to be self-dependent. She had learnt to live alone. Drew had freed her from the boredom of her home, the stultifying insistence of her parents that she live their sort of life. The smart socialising of her mother set her teeth on edge. Leona's occasional affairs, always with younger men with an eye to the main chance, had disgusted her. Marriage had opened her prison door and let her fly away, but if she gave herself to Drew now, she would find herself imprisoned in a misery she could not bear.

She could not even contemplate the prospect of becoming humiliatingly dependent on him. She felt self-disgust at her own weakness in even contemplating it.

She fell asleep with difficulty and when she woke in the morning she felt more like herself. She took time in dressing to re-establish her usual mask, the cool persona she was accustomed to seeing.

When she joined him, Drew was reading *Le Monde* as he drank his morning coffee. Over the top of the paper his grey eyes flicked over her face, narrowed in scrutiny which took in every visible clue as to her mood. He was wearing a tightly fitting, elegant pale blue suit with a shirt in a much darker shade of blue.

Helen gave him a cool nod and sat down, pouring

herself some coffee. She did not feel she could touch one of Madame Lefeuvre's flaky croissants. She dared not make even a pretence of eating. She might be shamed by real sickness. Her stomach was churning violently.

Drew's ironic, cynical stare told her that he had deciphered her face.

'What time do you expect Philip?' she asked civilly.

'He should be on the three o'clock flight,' Drew replied in the same tone. He folded *Le Monde* and placed it on the table, leaning his elbows on either side of his coffee cup, gazing at her.

'You look cool and collected.' There was derision in his smile. 'What are you doing this morning?'

She was very glad to be able to answer that. 'I have an appointment at eleven with the head vendeuse at Solange's. She assures me they have some clothes I shall love.'

'I have an appointment myself,' Drew returned. 'I'll drive you into town. Shall we lunch together?'

'I thought I might call Jeanne,' she said evasively.

'Jeanne and Raoul are in Lyons,' he said with smooth amusement. His eyes teased. 'Tough luck. You'll have to fall back on me.'

'I'm sure you could find one of your old flames to keep you amused,' she snapped, and at once wished she hadn't because his eyes narrowed with interested surprise on her face and she knew it had been a revealing remark.

'If I didn't know better,' Drew drawled, 'I'd call that the remark of a jealous woman.'

'You do know better,' she said dryly, her throat closing in alarm.

He held her eyes. 'So I do,' he murmured, but he had a strange little smile curling his mouth and she did not like the look of it.

She looked down, wishing that just once she could puncture that lazy self-confidence of his, see his smile wiped off his face. But he had had too many years in which to build up his self-assurance. Too many other women had fallen flat on their faces for him. Drew was impervious, secure in the knowledge of his own sex appeal.

He drove her to the salon and the thick streams of Paris traffic swam around the car, deafening her after the comparative quiet of London traffic. Horns blared, voices bellowed, tyres screeched. French drivers seemed to delight in noise. The sky was a halcyon, tender blue above the city, the familiar streets crowded. Watching Drew through her lashes obliquely as they halted at a traffic light, she saw a smile cross his face as a dark girl in a very tight red sweater and jeans sauntered across the road in front of their car. The girl turned and Helen caught her interested look at Drew in turn. Helen hurriedly averted her gaze, staring at a tall white building from which a tricolour drooped in windless sunshine. Damn him, she thought. Damn him!

The car moved on and she leaned back, watching his hands lightly manipulate the wheel. They were very long hands, sinewy, brown, the short dark hairs on the back of them merging into the tanned skin at a distance. They were very powerful hands. Helen had learnt their strength long ago, but last night as he fondled her she had for the first time learnt how delicate they could be when they chose, how sensitively they could move and what pleasure they could give.

He left her at the salon, reminding her that he would pick her up there at one, and vanished into the traffic. She found herself bored during her long session with the vendeuse; a small, spry, elegant dark woman with clever black eyes. Normally Helen enjoyed buying clothes, but today she had no room for anything in her head but Drew.

When she realised that, it gave her another shock. She had managed to escape the net of his sexual allure for years. Why was she falling into it like this now?

She pulled herself together and tried to concentrate on the clothes. One dress stood out among the rest. She had it called back and looked at it with pleasure.

Later, when Drew picked her up and asked how her morning had gone, she told him about the dress. 'I think you'll approve. It was rather more than I meant to pay, but it is special.'

'So long as you like it,' he said. 'I like you in white.' He gave her a wicked grin. 'So virginal.'

Helen flushed angrily and didn't answer.

He took her to a restaurant they both knew. The *patron* gave them a sly, interested look as he showed them to their table.

In the years of their marriage, Helen had learnt a little of Drew's family background. His own parents were both dead and he had no brothers or sisters. Once he had told her that he had a few scattered relatives but none whom he cared to visit. Helen had sympathised. She did not care for any of her family either. In a way, they had something in common; they were both used to self-sufficiency.

Looking across the table at this hard, sensual face, it occurred to her that it was extraordinary that after years

of marriage she should know so little of what happened inside his head. He was not a man who confided
his thoughts.

That was something else they had in common. Helen
was not famed for her confidences, either. She had a
number of friends, but only Janet had ever been close
enough for Helen to discuss anything intimate, and
even then it had never been anything about Drew.
Helen had accidentally found herself discussing her
father with Janet once, largely because Janet knew him
quite well. 'I've always been sorry for him,' Janet said.
'He works so hard and he feels it's all for nothing.'

Helen had been hurt by the frankness of that. Her
father's dismissal of her years ago had left a scar on
her. She had learnt to live with the fact that he felt
nothing but regret towards her, but she had not liked
hearing Janet state it so bluntly.

Looking at Drew now, she asked him suddenly:
'Does it make you feel good to know you've got a son to
inherit what you leave?'

His brows arched in the cynical dark face and the
grey eyes inspected her, narrowing. 'I really don't think
about it. I love Stephen because he's my son, but I hope
to God he can earn a living for himself without needing
to rely on what I leave him.'

'But you work very hard,' said Helen. 'Surely it
pleases you to believe that Stephen will carry on with
your business?'

'When I'm no longer running it, I don't give a damn
who, if anyone, is,' Drew shrugged. 'I work because I
enjoy it. I like building things. I've a constructive
nature. When I was a boy I used to make models of
planes and forts. I certainly don't stop to wonder what

will happen to the business when I'm not here.'

She frowned, looking down. It was a very different attitude from that of her father.

Drew was watching her shrewdly. 'Don't confuse me with Grey,' he said in a calm voice.

She looked up and their eyes met. 'It's ruined my father's life that I wasn't a boy.'

His mouth became straight and firm. 'Then he's a fool. In spending his time bewailing that he hasn't got a son, he's missed the point of life altogether.'

'What is the point of life?' she asked drily.

'Enjoying it,' said Drew.

Helen looked at him ironically. 'Of course—I'd forgotten.'

He eyed her, mockery coming into his face. 'You've never known,' he retorted.

'How do you know?' Her eyes flared angrily. 'What do you think you know about me?'

'I know this much, you've been shut in on yourself all your life because you think it's safer inside the four walls of your own mind. It isn't.' His eyes derisively underlined his words, his mouth straight and wry. 'It's far more dangerous. That's the road to neurotic depression.'

'Do I really seem depressed or neurotic?' she asked bitingly.

'Stephen saved you from that,' Drew replied.

She didn't answer, her face thoughtful. It was true. Stephen had been a lifeline to her, loving him had given her world meaning, purpose. She looked at Drew and away again. He had given her Stephen—forced her to bear him a son. For a long time she had felt nothing but icy bitterness about that, but from the first time she held Stephen in her arms she had loved him, and it had been a wonderful experience to love another human being for the first time. It had been like the removal of a great stone over her heart, releasing the fountain of love which circumstance had suppressed inside her.

Drew had been watching her closely, his eyes narrowed. 'Stephen has humanised you a little,' he commented. 'But you're still only half alive, aren't you?'

She met his eyes but could not read any message, explicit or otherwise, in those cool depths. There had always been a barrier between them, a large area of his mind unknown to her. He was not a man who displayed his thoughts—the charming mask he wore in company might deceive other people. It did not deceive Helen.

After their meal they drove to the airport to meet Philip. The drive was a pleasant one, sunshine glittering like spilt water on the road ahead of them. Drew played taped music as they drove, his body casually relaxed at the wheel, his eyes fixed ahead. The windows were wound down and cool air rushed over their faces, blowing Helen's hair into fine pale curls at the side of her head.

She got a white silk scarf out of her bag and tied it round her head, tucking the stray wisps of hair inside it. Drew gave her a brief glance, his brows lifting. 'I like it the way it was,' he told her. 'I so rarely see you dishevelled.' There was mocking irony in his eyes and Helen felt her face warming in response, colour rushing into her cheeks.

Looking away, she thought of her own response to him last night and hoped it had not made him imagine that she was a possible conquest.

Philip's tanned face stood out among the throng of

passengers as he came towards them. He walked with
a long stride, his shoulders back, head up, and when he
saw Helen with Drew his look of surprise was followed
immediately by one of unmistakable pleasure. He
turned to her at once as he met them, asking eagerly,
'Is Stephen with you?'

'No, he's in London,' she smiled.

His face fell. 'Oh, I brought him something. I meant
to fly on to London to give it to him.'

'Oh, you must,' she said warmly. 'He'd love to see
you. The giraffe is still his favourite toy. He takes it to
bed with him every night.'

'Is it?' Philip still hadn't looked at Drew. He was
staring at Helen with bright eyes. 'Has he grown
much?'

'He grows all the time,' she laughed.

'I would like to see him,' said Philip. With a little
start he turned to say wryly, 'Hi, Drew. Good of you to
meet me. I could have taken a taxi.'

'Not at all,' said Drew. 'The car's outside.' He
turned and strode off and Helen felt a quick dart of
intuition. Drew hadn't liked the fact that Philip had
showed such an interest in Stephen. She had never
noticed it before, but she wondered if he was possessive
towards his son. Following him, she and Philip talked
about the long flight which Philip had just undergone,
but while she listened to him she was watching the dark
head in front of them and pondering on the peculiarity
which Drew had just revealed to her. She knew from
the way he was walking that he was annoyed. There
was a suppressed rage in the set of his shoulders, the
lithe movements of his body. He walked, she thought,

as if he would like to stamp on something.

Gently she said, 'I'm sorry to hear about your wife, Philip.'

He glanced at her. 'Yes,' he said. 'Thank you.'

'I hadn't heard until yesterday. You should have come back to Europe sooner. You look tired.'

'It helped to go on working,' he said, looking away.

She slid her hand through his arm. 'Of course.'

He looked round at her, startled, then his arm closed on her hand, pressing it against him. 'You look very beautiful in that dress.'

She smiled at him. 'Thank you.' He wasn't a man who paid such compliments lightly and she valued it the more for that.

The ice-blue dress had been chosen deliberately with an eye to re-establishing her cool façade so far as Drew was concerned, but it did suit her, as she knew. The bodice was smooth and clung, the skirt was finely pleated, displacing as she moved to give a tantalising glimpse of her long legs. The colour underlined her gravely classical looks.

Arriving at the car she was put into it by Drew, his hand almost rough as he thrust her into her seat. Philip slid into the back and leaned back with a long sigh.

'It's good to be back in Europe.'

Turning in her seat, Helen surveyed him thoughtfully. 'You've lost a lot of weight. We must feed you up —lots of cream and steak!'

'Do you know what I really crave for?' Philip asked, breaking into a wry smile.

Drew flicked him an oblique, hard look. 'No,' he said drily. 'Tell us.'

Helen looked at him in surprise. He turned and started the ignition, the car bursting into a tigerish roar as he shot out of the parking space.

'Fish and chips,' Philip was saying, apparently unaware of Drew's little spurt of temper. 'In newspaper. With salt and vinegar from giant shakers.'

'You won't get that in Paris,' Helen laughed. 'The take-away here is Vietnamese. Rice with everything!'

Philip laughed, his teeth white against his dazzling tan. 'I'll have to wait until I get back to London, then.'

'What have you brought Stephen?' she asked, and her eyes smiled at him. 'Or would you rather keep it a secret?'

'A little construction kit of his own,' Philip said with a faint redness in his face.

She caught on, her eyes widening. 'You made it for him?'

He grimaced deprecatingly. 'With my own two hands. It gave me a kick—all shapes and sizes of wooden blocks and rods. I've designed them so that he can easily fit them together. They just slot into each other.' A faint shadow passed over his face. 'Do you think he'll like it?'

'He'll love it,' she said warmly. 'He takes after Drew. He uses his hands a lot.'

As she said that she felt the quick, derisive look Drew gave her and her head turned briefly to meet his eyes. She wished she hadn't looked at him the moment she had done so, but it was too late. Her face flushed delicately and she looked away at once.

A little huskily, she said to Philip, 'It's very good of you to take so much trouble for Stephen.'

'I enjoyed it.'

Philip had only met Stephen once, the day he brought the giraffe to their home. It touched her that he should have thought about the little boy, have gone to all the trouble of making him this toy.

'You're a born father,' she said, smiling, and wished she could have bitten her tongue out afterwards. Philip looked away, giving a polite little smile. Oh, God, why did I say that? she asked herself furiously. What a tactless, fatuous remark!

'You'll have to show Stephen how to use the kit,' she said hurriedly, to smooth over the awkward moment. 'I wouldn't have a clue and Drew's never at home.'

Drew changed gear noisily and the car shot up the side road leading to their apartment building.

When they got to the apartment Philip begged permission to have a shower because he was hot and tired after his flight. Helen went into her own bedroom to change and was just going to take off her dress when Drew walked into the room. She looked at him uncertainly, aware from the smouldering darkness of his face that he was still in a temper.

He stood with his hands pushed into his pockets, eyeing her grimly. 'Lay off Philip,' he said in a curt voice.

Helen was so taken aback she could only stare. After a moment she said incredulously, 'What?'

'You heard.'

'I heard,' she threw back fiercely, 'but I doubted my ears. What are you talking about?'

'The sweet smiles and fluttering eyelashes,' he said through his teeth. 'It may be calculated to goad me into losing my temper, but it could also lead to trouble you couldn't cope with, so lay off.'

Her face deeply flushed, Helen asked angrily, 'What are you accusing me of? Flirting? Don't be so absurd. Philip's a friend.'

He raised sardonic black brows. 'One you've only met very briefly once before, yet you encouraged him to kiss you at the airport.'

'On the cheek,' she retorted. 'What's so odd about that? He's been very kind to Stephen and he's just lost his wife.'

'Precisely,' Drew bit out. 'He's vulnerable at the moment. One too many of your sweet smiles and he could go nuts over you, which would do neither of you any good in the long run. You're nowhere near hand-ling an adult relationship yet and Philip probably never will be.'

'By adult,' she said coldly, 'I presume you mean an affair?'

'Call it what you like,' Drew said tersely. 'You couldn't cope with it. The two of you would merely drown in a sticky mess and someone else would be left to clear up the debris. I've no wish to be landed with that job.'

'Get out of my room,' she said raggedly, 'before I hit you.'

He moved closer, staring into her angry face. 'Just remember this, Philip's a damned good engineer and an old friend of mine. I don't want him broken up by another destructive relationship. He took enough from the little bitch he married.'

'What makes you think I'd hurt him?' she asked with a long bitter stare at him.

'You couldn't help it,' Drew told her unpleasantly. 'The way you're made, you'd tear him into shreds.'

The cruelty of that sent all the colour from her face. Aghast, she stared at him. 'What a vile thing to say!'

'It's the truth,' Drew grated. 'Philip is like a car without an engine at the moment. He's lost all sense of purpose. I saw him looking at you and I read his mind. He doesn't know you. He's fooled by the cool, quiet manner. The fact that you have a child makes you doubly attractive to him. What he's desperately in need of at the moment is a warm, loving woman, and he might just be stupid enough to believe you're one.'

The insult brought hot colour rushing back into her face, her hands tightly balled into fists at her sides. She was so angry that she couldn't speak, staring at him with flashing eyes, their blue intensified almost to a purple.

Drew put his head to one side, regarding her with heavy irony. 'Lost for words?'

'What do you expect me to say? I'm not going to defend myself against a remark like that one.'

His mouth twisted. 'I imagine there's a man somewhere who could get through to you, but it wouldn't be Philip. All you could do for him is drive him right off his rocker, and I won't have it.'

'I've no interest in Philip in that way,' she protested angrily. 'I was merely polite to him.'

'You smiled at him,' Drew said oddly. 'Don't you know how rarely you smile, and almost never at a man?'

Helen stared, incredulous.

'And when you smile your face comes to life,' Drew went on flatly. 'I told you yesterday, you're twice as lovely when you smile, and twice as dangerous to a romantic like Philip.'

'I wouldn't hurt him,' she whispered drily. 'How could I?'

'Just by being yourself,' Drew retorted. 'Cold, untouchable and as remote as a star. Philip needs someone a bit more human than you.'

She winced at the description. In all honesty, she recognised it as a description which could fit. Her self-protective barriers had been designed to keep pain at bay but no doubt to other people she might well seem cold and inhuman. Drew, in particular, had been held at a safe distance from her since they met, but only because she was aware that Drew could hurt her if she let him come too close. Last night he had come closer than he ever had before, though.

He caught the flicker in her eyes, and his smile became pointed and sardonic. 'Oh, yes, last night you came down off that star, but you soon flew off again, didn't you? You found human company a little too red-blooded for you. You breathe a more rarefied atmosphere up there in the polar wastes you call your life.'

'I've more self-respect than to let you use me for one of your one-night stands,' she retorted thickly.

The grey eyes flashed. He moved to the door at a stride. 'Remember, just play it cool with Philip.'

'Or what?' she taunted, knowing she risked reprisals but feeling a strange, excited pleasure in knowing she had somehow flicked his ego.

For a moment she thought he was coming back. He swung, stiffening, and his face had a strange, taut look, then he said grimly, 'Or I'll teach you to be frightened of me, Helen.'

The door slammed. She found herself trembling at the way he had said that. He hadn't touched her, yet she was frightened already. Drew could be very alarming when that harsh note came into his voice. His strength could be charged with menace if he chose. She had never realised before that under that lazy charm of his he could be so dangerous. From the first day they met he had teased, mocked, laughed at her. The laziness had been absent from his face just now. She had been seeing the man who ran his business with a ruthless hand.

She remembered her father talking about Drew once and remarking on these contradictions in his nature. The man who had built up his firm to its present position was not the man who lounged casually around the houses of his friends, relaxed and charming. She had just seen the Drew who could cut throats without flinching. He was tough, and he meant her to know it. He wouldn't hesitate to carry out his threat if he thought she was encouraging Philip.

She hadn't consciously been flirting with Philip; her manner to him had been pleasant and friendly, perhaps, but it was only in contrast to her usual coolness that Drew had seen it as flirtation. Philip had made a distinct and warm impression on her at their other meeting. Stephen was the only important thing in her life and Philip's rapport with him had touched her. Also, she had been sorry to hear of Philip's wife's death; shocked by Drew's revelations about the failure of that marriage. Philip had had a bad time and Helen was sorry for him. Anything else had been in Drew's imagination.

She thought of his biting remarks about her and winced again, her face shadowed.

It might be justifiable criticism, but it hurt to be

described as inhuman, untouchable, even if it was an image of herself she had quite deliberately projected to him. No one could enjoy being shown such a portrait of themselves, having a mirror held up to their nature which showed it in such painful detail. Staring at herself in her dressing-table mirror, she shivered. Had the mask she had worn for most of her life become the real person underneath? Had it grown into her flesh?

CHAPTER FOUR

AFTER their marriage, it had surprised and touched Helen to find that Drew had provided all their homes with good pianos so that whatever part of the world she might be in, she would always be able to play. She still spent at least two hours a day at the piano. They were periods of restful concentration, absorbing hours when she was free in the only way she ever felt really free. Drew had insisted that she resume tuition, as well, although he would not allow her to take full-time musical education.

'It would take up too much of your life,' he said, and after Stephen's birth she had in any case lost the urge to follow music as a career. As soon as Stephen could sit on her lap she had begun to teach him to enjoy the piano, making it a game which the little boy adored. She used to tell him stories to which her music formed a background, playing like a pianist at a silent film, scary creepy music for a story about the big bad wolf or light dancing music for a fairy story.

Now, after dinner, Philip asked her to play for him. 'Drew tells me you're very good.'

She gave Drew a brief glance and he bowed mockingly, his lips wry. Helen got up and went to the piano. Guessing at Philip's tastes, she chose to play a romantic piece of Chopin. She had left her hair down tonight on impulse, brushing it into a loose silky fall down her shoulders, holding it back behind her nape with a diamond bow which Drew had given her.

Far below, the roar of Paris traffic had been muted by the night. The music spilled out into a listening silence. Philip leaned back on the couch and stared around the room. Helen had made it elegant, in the restrained fashion she admired, marked by splashes of colour and excitement—a Chinese vase in a smooth bronze green, the tapestry on the wall with its vivid blue fish and scarlet poppies, the harlequin colours of the satin cushions. Philip's eyes wandered from one to the other and then came back to Helen.

Drew was smoking a cigar, his eyes narrowed, glancing from Philip to Helen occasionally, and back again. The watchful cast of his face was hard to read.

Helen was wearing a coral silk dress which had an almost sculptured look; folding, Greek fashion, over her breasts and falling in a gentle line to her feet, tied at her waist by a thin plaited belt of gold. In the lamplight her face was softened by the loose pale glitter of her hair. The music touched her features into tranquil beauty, almost tenderness, and there was warmth in her smile as she ended and turned to look at the two men.

Music always altered her mood, sinking into the fertile soil of her mind and changing her. Cool and reflective otherwise, she was deeply responsive to music, coloured by it.

'Drew hit the nail on the head,' said Philip in oddly husky tones. 'You're fantastic. You should be doing it professionally.'

Drew stared at his cigar tip, the glowing redness moving as he flicked ash into an ashtray.

Helen half smiled, half sighed. 'Once I might have wanted to, but I doubt if one can combine a career in music with a child. I'd have to see far less of Stephen, and I'd hate that.' She laughed. 'So would Stephen!'

'Of course,' Philip said seriously. 'I forgot. And you don't regret giving up the chance of fame and fortune, Helen?'

She looked surprised. 'No, not at all. I have more than enough money already, and as to fame ...' she shrugged, 'I wouldn't want that, anyway. Music to me is its own reward. I need no other.'

Philip stared at her as she half turned to pick idly at the keys, her slender neck bent, the silken gleam of her hair falling sideways to expose more of the white nape.

Drew stubbed out his cigar with a rough movement and said drily, 'You used to play, didn't you, Philip?'

Helen looked round, surprised. 'Did you?' She rose, the silk sliding down over her body with a soft rustle. 'Do play for us, Philip.'

'After that? Not likely!' Philip was pink and grinning. 'Drew meant I bang out some music hall songs occasionally. Out in Africa, the men will listen to anyone, however lousy.'

Helen sat down again, patting the stool beside her. 'Come and play Chopsticks.'

Laughing, he joined her and they had fun playing Chopsticks for a few moments, before Helen slid into playing an easy medley of comic songs with which Philip was able to join her. Philip sang as he thumped out the music. He had a pleasant baritone, hitting the notes nicely.

She looked sideways at him thoughtfully. 'You must be a boon to your workmates out in Africa. A concert party laid on every night!'

He looked sheepish. 'Oh, they put up with me now and again, when they're desperate.'

'It must be dull for them out there.'

'Fairly tedious,' he agreed. 'They drink a lot, especially in that terrible heat.'

'Don't you get fed up with the life, Philip?'

His bronzed face was sober. 'Pretty often,' he admitted. 'Sometimes I long to come home, but then I wouldn't earn half as much back in England. I hardly pay any tax at all out there, you see, and living expenses are very low.' He smiled at her, his eyes on the enormous blue eyes beneath their fine brows. 'It helped to have that construction kit to work on for the last few months.'

She was touched, smiling back at him. 'I've been teaching Stephen to play lately,' she told him.

'Really? Does he like the piano?'

'Loves it. His fingers are stubby at the moment, but he likes making noises, the louder the better.' She imitated Stephen's thudding little hands on the keys and Philip roared with amusement.

'He and I would make a great pair, then. We could play duets.'

'You must get him to show you when you come to London. If you're still coming.'

'I'd like to,' Philip said with a husky note in his voice, glancing away from her. She felt a quiver of warning and involuntarily turned her head. Drew sat with arms folded, his face grim, the look in his eyes making her shiver.

As though Philip, too, became aware of Drew's presence and his anger, he rose, his face flushed. 'Well,' he said nervously, 'I'm tired. If you'll excuse me, I think I'll make an early night of it.'

When he had gone Drew regarded her with dangerous eyes. 'I warned you,' he said very softly.

Helen stood facing him, her body trembling under the silky material of the coral dress, her hands clenched at her sides. 'I wasn't doing it deliberately,' she broke out. 'I like him. What do you want me to do? Ignore him?'

'You've managed to hand men off easily enough before.'

'Philip's different.'

'He's more vulnerable,' Drew snapped.

'That's why,' she said helplessly. 'I don't want to hurt him.'

Drew's eyes narrowed and he watched her relentlessly. 'You realise that you could, then.'

'He's open to hurt,' she said in a confused mutter. 'That's what's so appealing about him.'

'Yes,' Drew said oddly, staring at her in that fixed way. 'And you've never been open to emotion of any kind, have you, Helen? Except for Stephen I suspect you've never let yourself care for anyone.'

She did not answer, her eyes falling away from him.

'Has anyone ever cared for you?' Drew asked then, very quietly.

Helen smiled, shaking her head, and her smile was ironic. 'Except Stephen,' she added.

'Ah, yes, Stephen,' he said. A bright mockery invaded his stare. 'Yet I had to force him on to you.'

Her face ran with angry colour and she looked at

him furiously. 'You don't have to remind me!'

'I'm sure I don't,' he agreed, rising.

She took a step backward and Drew laughed. Something in that laughter made the hair rise on the back of her neck. He raised one dark eyebrow in sardonic comment.

'Why are you so jumpy, Helen?'

She didn't answer, looking away. Drew walked towards her and she would have fled if she hadn't forced herself to stand still, refusing to panic. He had threatened to make her frightened of him if she flirted with Philip again. She was not sure exactly what he had meant, but she was already frightened.

'Scared?' he asked in a taunting whisper.

'No,' she lied, lifting her head to glare at him.

'Liar,' he breathed, smiling. His fingers slid sensuously over her bare arm, lingering on her elbow where a pulse was going fiercely, the little blue flicker of her vein visible.

'What are you going to do?' she challenged. 'Beat me?' She smiled to show her contemptuous defiance and Drew smiled back, his eyes gleaming.

'Don't tempt me.'

Helen flushed, her eyes falling restlessly. The fingertips on her arm were making her feel breathless, deeply aware of him.

'Leave me alone,' she said desperately.

He put his hand up to her hair and deftly undid the diamond bow. She caught the glitter of the stones as he pushed it into his jacket pocket, then he delicately arranged her hair over her shoulders in a silken fan, his fingertips brushing her bare shoulders. 'I like your hair loose, it makes you look more feminine. When you drag it back off your face, you look like an affronted Victorian.'

She swallowed nervously, very aware of the way he was looking at her. The smouldering anger had gone from his face and now he was smiling slightly, his eyes half-closed as he looked at her.

'I thought you might thaw a little over the years,' he said softly, 'but the ice gets thicker every time I see you. If I leave it much longer I'll have to use a sledge-hammer.'

Confused, she stared up at him, trying to read his face. 'What are you talking about?'

'You wouldn't know, even if I told you,' said Drew with a twist of that hard mouth. 'Life, Helen—what happens outside that head of yours, the thing you've been running from for years.'

She took a painful breath. 'If this is another attempt to get me to sleep with you, forget it. I don't want to know.'

'I realise that,' Drew said sardonically. 'But I'm your husband. It's time you came to terms with the fact.'

'Our marriage only exists on paper!'

'That can be altered.' His eyes glinted.

'I won't get involved in one of your games,' she said hoarsely. 'I know you like sophisticated amusements, but count me out.'

'This is no game,' he said, his voice husky. His hands went to her waist, drawing her towards him, and she was so surprised by the uneven note in his tone that she went unresistingly. She realised as she swayed against him that that had surprised him, too. His eyes glittered more brightly, then his body was pressed against her, and she felt pulses begin to beat at her wrists, her throat, her temples. She put her hands against his chest in protest, lifting her head, and he looked at her in challenge.

'Last night you came to life for a moment, Helen. It was a short visit, but I think you found it more enjoyable than you'd imagined you would.'

She shook her head dumbly and he smiled with a dry movement of his mouth. 'Oh, yes,' he whispered. 'Do you think I didn't know?'

Her breath caught. She couldn't look away from him, her eyes wide and glazed.

'It frightened you, didn't it?' he asked softly. 'You're so afraid of the water that you won't learn to swim, but you can't stay out of life for ever, Helen.' His hands moved down her back, following the curve of her spine, pressing her towards him.

'You're very plausible, Drew, but I won't let you seduce me,' she said bitterly. 'I'm not making one of your occasional bedfellows.'

He moved backwards, pulling her with him. She tried to get away as she realised his intention, but Drew imposed his strength on her without remorse, his fingers biting into her. He sank down on to the couch and she found herself on his lap, his arms round her waist, restraining her as she tried to get away.

'Stop it! I won't,' she muttered incoherently.

Drew's hands moved deftly and she found herself tilted back against his arm, her head turned up towards him. He looked down at her, a smile on his mouth, a small, teasing smile which was reflected in the grey eyes.

'Isn't it cold, Helen?'

She was puzzled by the question, her brows drawing

together. 'Cold?' It was a warm summer evening and
he disconcerted her by asking that.

The long, sensual mouth turned up at the edges. His
eyes danced. She felt his hand on her back. He was
pulling down the zip on her dress.

'No!' she broke out huskily, wriggling.

'Aren't you tired of that star yet?' he asked softly.
'Don't you find it cold and lonely up there?' His fingers
moved on her naked back, the tips gently tingling
along her spine. She felt them playing with the fine
golden hairs scattered along the curve of her back,
brushing the hairs down, raising them again with a light
touch. A little shiver ran through her.

Drew bent his black head and she shrank back, but
there was no violence in him. His lips descended
against her eyes, closing them, softly playing with the
lids, tickling over her flickering lashes.

Her dress slid down over her arms. She tried to look
at him and he kissed her eyes shut again. 'Please,' she
whispered shakily.

She felt his lips smiling as they brushed over her lids.

'You may like sensual games. I don't,' she said
angrily.

Drew laughed. 'Do you know what you're saying?
What do you imagine sensuality is, Helen?'

'I don't want to know!' She put her hands against
his shoulders, pushing at him.

He took both her wrists and yanked them backwards,
tethered her deftly with one hand, her arms behind
her neck. She was bent over his arm and his mouth
came down on her throat, delicately tickling her skin.
She tried to open her eyes, but somehow the light hurt
them.

'Sensuality is the world perceived through the senses, Helen. What do you think we were given our five senses for? To feel, to touch, to taste, to see.'

His kiss was on the pulsing hollow at the base of her throat and she knew he must be aware of that pulse quickening at his touch. Her body was betraying her and she couldn't do a thing about it.

'There's nothing wrong with your senses, Helen. They're in good working order. Your ear is perfect. Your taste in clothes, art, perfume, is educated and sensitive. You have the right equipment, Helen. It's time you learnt how to use it.'

His hand was sliding up her back and she gave a cry of angry alarm as she realised what he was doing. Deftly he was unhooking her bra.

She felt the give the moment when his fingers achieved their aim. Drew's head bowed with a little gasp and his lips touched her exposed breasts. Her back arched and she gave a muffled cry, remembering her wedding night, the burning touch of his mouth as he explored her body. She had not wanted to remember. She had tried to forget. But at the back of her head all these years that sharp impression had remained, the hungry touch of Drew's mouth against her body.

Drew raised his head. There was a little silence. She opened her eyes, her face dazed. He stared at her strangely, his eyes piercing her face. Helen couldn't move. Her lips parted on a breathless surprise, she stared back at him. He slowly bent his head and his mouth settled on her own. She felt her hands released. As if Drew's will urged them upward, her arms curved and were round his neck. Drew groaned against her lips. 'Yes, Helen, yes,' he whispered.

The kiss consumed her. She clung, shuddering, meeting the heat of his mouth with a heat of her own, her hands feeling the rough black hair tingling against her palms and fingertips.

He moved back at last and Helen stared at him feverishly. 'I want you, Helen,' he told her huskily. 'But this time I'm not forcing anything from you. This time you're going to give and until you're ready to give, I shall wait. Don't make me wait too long.'

He slowly drew up her zip, pulling her dress back around her. His hands brushed her hair back over her shoulders. He lifted her like a child and sat her on the couch.

His manner changed. 'Tell me about James Farrier,' he said, taking her by surprise yet again.

Helen blinked, too shaken by what had just happened to pull her thoughts together. 'James? What about him? I told you, he's the accountant who looks after the agency.'

'And does he want to look after you too?'

The cynical question made her flush. 'No,' she retorted, although she was not exactly telling the truth since she suspected James did not find her unattractive, but there had never been anything but the utmost circumspection between them.

'Stephen's jealous of him,' Drew observed.

'Jealous?' Her voice rose and she flushed. 'Nonsense!' She knew her face was burning and wanted to put her hands to it but would not let herself do anything so betraying.

'Oh, yes,' Drew drawled. 'He naïvely told me as much. He complained that "Uncle James" came to see

you all the time and Stephen doesn't like him.' He
turned a mocking eye on her. 'He also asked me why I
didn't come home more often. He sounded very reproachful. Other boys, he told me, had daddies who
were home all the time.'

She was horrified. 'Stephen said that?'

'He's growing up,' Drew explained. 'He's beginning
to notice things. He may only be a little boy, but he
has sound instincts and he guesses at the danger to himself when a man visits you too often.'

'James only comes on business!'

'Stephen sees it as a threat. Does Farrier like him?'

Helen hesitated and Drew's brows lifted.

'No, I thought not,' he nodded.

'If James isn't exactly fond of him it's Stephen's own
fault. He bit James.'

Drew roared, his eyes filled with laughter. 'Did he,
indeed? Well, well. A boy of sound instincts, as I said.
I wish I'd been there.'

Helen felt her lips quivering. 'James was horrified.
I think he suspected Stephen was unhinged. Nothing
like that ever happened to him before.'

Drew eyed her mockingly. 'I wonder why Stephen
bit him.'

She looked away. 'James annoyed him, that's all. It
took me ages to calm James down. I'm sure he went off
to get a tetanus injection afterwards.'

'My God! Is that the sort of man he is? Your taste
is suspect, Helen.'

'He's my accountant, not ...' She broke off, biting
her lower lip, her eyes evading him.

'Not your lover?' Drew laughed softly. 'You don't
have to tell me that. You've never had a lover.'

She was stung and looked at him furiously. 'Don't be so sure.'

His amusement was infuriating. 'I'm certain,' he drawled. 'I'd bet everything I own on it.' The long fingers reached out to touch her hot cheek. 'Wake up, Helen. You're no longer happy on that remote star of yours.'

'What makes you think that?' she asked because she wondered why he was suddenly making this determined attack on her. Why now? They had been married for years and he had never tried to make love to her before. Why was he behaving like this now?

He took the question seriously. 'Like Stephen, I have sound instincts. I got a hunch when I was talking to him on the phone. From what he said, I guessed Farrier might be interested in you and I wanted to know if there'd been any change in the status quo.'

Helen stared at him, wide-eyed. 'What are you talking about?'

'I've been a weather man for six years, Helen,' he said with a crooked little grin. 'I've become very expert at reading the signs. When pack ice starts to break up one has to act fast.'

Helen felt her heart thudding. 'Why do you talk in riddles?' she asked in a husky, nervous little voice.

He laughed. 'Why don't you bring Stephen out to Kowoli when I go back?'

The change of subject threw her. After a moment she said: 'I don't somehow see myself living on the site with all your men.'

'I'd take a house for you and Stephen, of course,' he said with smooth amusement.

'Did you mention this to him?'

He caught her suspicious glance and shook his head. 'I don't think you can accuse me of going behind your back, Helen. I wouldn't involve Stephen in our struggle.'

'What struggle?'

He looked at her drily and she looked away.

'All the same, I think it would be a good idea for Stephen to come out and see where I work, how I live.'

'I should have realised he was worrying about it,' Helen said in self-accusation. She had thought she knew everything about her son. They were so close, and yet Stephen had had this on his mind and never mentioned it to her. The revelation that Stephen had thoughts of which she knew nothing disturbed and upset her.

'Children tend to hide their deeper feelings,' Drew soothed. 'Don't be upset about it.'

'I am upset. I should have guessed. He's very attached to you.'

'Attached? Funny word to use. Do you mean my son loves me, and is that so strange?'

'Of course not. It's very natural.'

'But it surprises you.'

'Stephen hasn't seen much of you, after all.'

'Thanks to you!'

Her eyes flew to his face in shock and anger. 'That isn't fair. I've never stopped you seeing him.'

'Last year I was in London seven times. I only saw Stephen twice, and even then it was only because I took the precaution of bringing guests with me so that you would stay in London. If I'd arrived on my own, you and Stephen would have been out of the country before I got there.'

'That was our agreement!'

'I never agreed to be a stranger to my son, only to you.'

Helen looked at him in consternation. 'No,' she said at last. 'Now that Stephen is growing up, perhaps he could come to stay with you.'

'My God! You're so predictable! A duty visit once a year, I suppose? Just Stephen, never you. Can't you get it through that stupid little head of yours that what the boy needs is a family? A mother and a father who care for him? Just because your parents never gave a twopenny damn for you it doesn't mean the same thing has to happen to Stephen.'

Her blue eyes glittered with unshed tears, her face stricken. 'You have no right to say that! I care for Stephen! I love him and he loves me.'

'And that must be enough for him, must it? Do you resent the fact that he wants me, too, Helen?'

'No,' she cried bitterly. 'No! Of course not. I told you, it's natural enough. Do you really think I'd deny him anything he wants and needs?'

'And what about your needs?' Drew asked, watching her disturbed and troubled face.

'Mine?' She looked at him with wide, tear-filled eyes.

'Do you really imagine you don't have any?' His mouth twisted in a dry smile. 'Oh, you've crushed them out of sight for years, but you're human, Helen. You have them all right.'

'Not any you would understand,' she said bitterly.

'Try me.' He watched her with level grey eyes.

'Your instincts are sound, you said,' Helen bit out.

'Animal instincts, Drew. I don't want to know about them.'

'Human beings are animals,' Drew told her coolly. 'Sorry to shatter your illusions, Helen, but you're an animal yourself. You may try to suppress those healthy animal instincts, but they can't be killed. When you touch something, whether it's a flower or a knife and fork, you're using your fingertips as sensory devices. You feel everything you touch, Helen. When a baby is learning, it puts everything in its mouth because the mouth is a sensitive instrument and can tell it about the shape, the taste, the density of what it holds.' He moved closer and bent his head to touch his mouth to her bare arm. She shivered and Drew lifted his head, a dry smile on his lips.

'Yes, you felt that. I felt it. We shared an experience, an animal experience. One which gave both of us pleasure.'

She silently shook her head, angry because she knew she was lying. The warm brush of his lips had given her pleasure.

Drew's grey eyes told her he knew she lied. 'We go on using our mouths to discover the nature of what we see, Helen.' He slowly ran his glance down over her and she tensed, shuddering. 'It can be a very exciting experience.'

'None of this has anything to do with Stephen!'

He looked amused. 'No? I think it has. I remember when Stephen was a baby how you used to have him on your lap after his bath, tickling his toes. He enjoyed it. You enjoyed it. Oh, yes, Helen, deny your needs to yourself, but don't try to deny them to me.'

'I would never deny my love for Stephen.'

'Do you still hold it against me because I made you have him?'

She looked away, shaking her head. How could she regret it when it had resulted in the life of the one human being with whom she had ever had a warm relationship?

'I'm sorry I had to use force,' Drew told her flatly. 'Believe me, I regretted the necessity. I tried not to hurt you any more than I had to, but some pain was inevitable.'

'You lied to me when you promised our marriage wouldn't be a real one!'

'Not in the beginning. I never intended what happened. Your father made it necessary by insisting on grandchildren.'

She moved restlessly. 'I'd rather not talk about it. It wasn't an experience I enjoyed.' Her eyes were sarcastic as she looked at him. 'Despite your talk about the value of animal experiences!'

His eyes narrowed. 'Of course you couldn't enjoy it—you were frigid and ice-cold. You refused to let me near you. You've matured since then, though; you're a woman, not a frozen girl. Wake up to your own needs before it's too late, Helen.'

She felt a flare of rebellious rage. 'And what makes you think my needs would include you?'

She caught the brief flash in his eyes, then he smiled, mockery entering his face. 'You need what I can give you and you've told me yourself that there's nobody else.'

'Not yet,' she said softly.

Drew stared at her, his brows drawn harshly over the grey eyes. For a moment she felt a thrust of fear at something in his face, then the expression dissolved into the familiar mockery.

'We'll see,' he drawled. He got up and walked to the door. Turning, he surveyed her with a calm, passionless face. 'Join the human race, Helen. You aren't happy any more on your cold star. Admit that and come down to earth.'

When he had gone, Helen stared at the closed door with a fast-beating heart. Join the human race, become vulnerable and open to hurt? She didn't know if she had the nerve, or whether, if she did, she might not be scarred by the experience and left worse off than she was now.

What was Drew trying to do? Seduce her? She might be innocent, but she was not totally stupid. She was not allowing him to enmesh her in his seductive net of male allure, however tempted she might be by the experienced movements of those long hands.

She could not deny even to herself that he had given her a heady taste of the pleasure he could offer. However much she hated the admission Drew had made her head spin while he was making love to her. That wasn't so surprising. He had had plenty of experience.

That was what held her back, that was what always came between them, Drew was too calculating. He knew what he was doing all the time. The seductive hands were controlled by a cool brain. He never lost control of himself.

He might call her inhuman, but what was he? A machine for making love? She did not doubt that he enjoyed lovemaking. She had felt the pleasure in his body as he caressed her, but his pleasure had been as deliberate as his other actions. He had even been controlling that.

She felt a strange, burning desire to make him lose control, to jam the instrument panel in that head of his and see his cool face without the customary glint of awareness in his eyes. Had that ever happened to him? she wondered. Had he ever gone crazy? Or had that mind always been in charge of every act, every movement he made?

CHAPTER FIVE

IT was a surprise to Helen that she slept well that night. When she woke up she found Drew in her mind as though he had already been there while she slept. Her body stretched, sensuous and lazy, under the fine lemon sheets and she curved her arms above her head and stared at the curtains, watching the pale slide of the light coming through them. She felt no urge to get up. Below, the Paris traffic surged like the tide, but in the quiet bedroom Helen felt luxuriously idle, unwilling to move. One human experience Drew had not included in his list of sensuous pleasures had been sleep, she thought drily. Yet it was one of the most enjoyable experiences in the world to wake after a deep sleep. What happened to the mind and body during sleep? A faint colour invaded her face as she thought the question. What travels did the mind take when it was freed from the inhibitions of the day?

She flung back her covers and jumped out of bed, preferring not to follow that thought through. She had a little suspicion that her mind had betrayed her last night in sleep. She had gone to bed aroused and tense. She could not remember her dreams, but she knew very well that she had had them.

Under the shower she turned with closed eyes and a face lifted to the water, smiling to herself. Another of life's sensuous pleasures, she thought. Was the list endless? The water danced on her warm skin and trickled down her face like tears. Her head raised, she pushed back wet strands of hair and turned to step over to get her towel.

It was put into her hand as she groped for it and her eyes flew open in shock.

Drew leaned on the cubicle frame, his broad shoulders filling the space between the glass doors. Helen felt her heart rise into her throat and for a moment she could neither move nor speak.

Drew's eyes wandered in leisurely inspection over the naked wet curve of shoulder, breast and thigh, and she was so taken aback that she did not even move to cover her body. The water still sluiced down her back, ran down between her toes. The full, rounded breasts seemed to ache heavily, her nipples hardening under the grey eyes. She had never in her life been so conscious of her body and yet so frozen in any ability to make it act. Drew's stare immobilised her as though she gave him licence to look where he chose. And he chose to see everything, his face unrevealing, moving from the fine bones of her shoulders down over the smooth flesh of her breasts, her tight waist and the damp pale plateau beneath.

He drew a breath and she came out of her trance and flung the towel around herself, her teeth beginning to chatter, as though she were chilled.

'What the hell do you think you're doing?' That couldn't be her own voice, she thought, that rough, shaking sound coming from her lips.

'Philip and I are just off,' he said coolly. 'I came in to tell you we'd be out all day at this factory. We'll be back for dinner.'

'Don't ever come in here again,' she said rustily. She

turned her back on him to stop the shower, her towel firmly covering her, and Drew moved. She felt him behind her and was about to swing round when his hands went round her body and his mouth nuzzled the damp nape of her neck before it slipped very slowly down her back. His fingers spread over her breasts, pressing the towel against her.

'Shrew,' he muttered. Then he abruptly whipped the towel from her and she gasped in rage as she felt the sting of his hand on her. He laughed, dropping the towel, then walked off, leaving her raging helplessly. The slap had not been violent, but it had been infuriating. Her towel was soaked, lying in the floor of the shower. Angrily she heard Drew slam her bedroom door. She walked out of the shower naked and stared at herself in the long mirror.

Her own hands came up and curved over her full breasts. She closed her eyes.

I want him, she thought. Does he know?

While he was staring at her, she had enjoyed it. A hot colour ran into her face as she faced that: she had enjoyed it. His face had not told her anything, yet she had felt the rise of desire in him and had instinctively reacted to it. For the first time in her life she had been conscious of power, the power of her own body. Ever since she met him she had been aware of Drew's power, the male allure with which he was so clever, spreading it like the multi-coloured tail of a peacock so that it caught the female eye. Now she began to know what an effect her own body could have.

Swallowing, she turned away from her own reflection and began to get ready for the day. When she went in to breakfast Madame Lefeuvre gave her a quick, searching little glance, a smile hovering on her lips.

Helen told her that she was going out and that there would be three of them to dinner.

'Ah, a great pity,' Madame sighed, her eyes sliding to wink at Helen. 'Two is a more comfortable number.'

Helen ignored that. She gave her orders for the meal and sat down to drink some coffee, then went off to finish her shopping.

She lunched alone and found herself far more aware than ever before of the occasional male glance. It annoyed her to notice. She frowned over her meal. Drew was altering the whole structure of her nature and she found it frightening. She had spent years in building her wall to keep the world out and now he was loosening it brick by brick.

Or had it started to crumble long ago? Had it begun on the night he forced her to submit to him, despite her angry useless protests? What had happened that night had been like a time bomb planted in her flesh. It had not exploded at the time. It had lain waiting inside her for its moment of detonation, the fusing of the right elements to cause the final explosion.

It had happened now, though, she recognised. Hard to say when—perhaps the moment she saw him in the airport, perhaps later when he kissed her that first evening, or last night when he sensuously caressed her. Or all those moments had come together as she stood naked in the shower and Drew's cool eyes made that leisurely voyage over her.

Her safety wall had crashed and she was wide open to him. But did he know?

'Helen!'

The voice brought her head up and she smiled in pleasure as she recognised Jeanne.

'Drew told me you and Raoul were in Lyons!'

'We were,' Jeanne agreed, seating herself opposite Helen at the table. 'Raoul had to come back to Paris for a board meeting and I decided to come, too. You should have let me know you were coming over—we could have lunched together. How long are you staying?' Then her brown eyes narrowed. 'Drew, did you say? Is he here too?'

Helen's face tightened slightly. 'Yes,' she said unrevealingly. 'We're both at the apartment.'

Jeanne was older, in her thirties, a short dark woman with a clever sophisticated face and eyes which had yellow specks among the brown. Her hair was crisp and curled around her face in well-trained neatness.

'And Stephen?' Jeanne probed.

'He's in London.'

'*Vraiment?*' Jeanne smiled and Helen looked away. She had met Jeanne four years ago when Raoul brought his wife to London for some sort of business trip. Raoul was a close friend of Drew's. They dined at a fashionable London restaurant together, then Raoul and Jeanne were guests at Helen's dinner table. Several times since she had met Jeanne in Paris for lunch or dinner. They got on well, although they were not intimate.

Jeanne was far too discreet to ask questions about Helen's marriage, but they knew each other well enough for Helen to guess that Jeanne was aware of something of the hollowness of the relationship between Helen and Drew. Jeanne's own marriage to

Raoul was ideal, a close warm marriage which had resulted in two sons.

'How are Pierre and Louis?' Helen asked now, and Jeanne replied a little drily.

'Very well, thank you. And Stephen?'

'Very well. Growing fast.'

'Don't they all?' The waiter brought the coffee and Jeanne asked him to bring another cup. 'A pity we have both lunched alone.' She gave a typical Gallic shrug, her face grimacing. 'I find it a bore to eat alone—that is why I came out. Raoul is off to lunch with his directors and I knew I would end up with a lettuce leaf if I stayed at home alone. Too much of a chore to cook for oneself.' She smiled at Helen. 'My housekeeper is with the boys at our place in Provence. You know, you and Drew should bring Stephen over there one week. The boys could play together—it would do Stephen good to have company.' Her brown eyes held a smile. 'He is too much alone with you. It will spoil him.'

'It's very kind of you to ask us. I'm sure Stephen would love to play with the boys.'

'Louis is just a year older than him. They would get on well. Boys like each other's company. Like young animals, they like to fight and quarrel. It is a trial of strengths, a locking of horns.' Jeanne's face held cynical amusement. 'Boys grow into men, remember.'

'And men love to lock horns,' Helen muttered wryly.

Jeanne grinned wickedly. 'Especially men like Drew.'

Helen laughed and looked down into her coffee, but her laughter had a hollow ring. Jeanne eyed her speculatively.

'*Tout va bien*, Helen?'

'Oh, everything's fine,' Helen lied, but Jeanne looked unconvinced. Her gaze surveyed Helen thoughtfully.

'I guess it is not always easy with a man like Drew. I've known him a long time. Before he married you, he had quite a name.'

Helen grimaced. '*Before* he married me?' Her tone was bitter. 'Don't tell me anything has changed.'

Jeanne sat up, her coffee cup between her hands, her eyes sharp. '*Chérie?* Something is wrong. Is it *une poule?*'

Helen's mouth twisted at the expression. 'Not any particular one, I imagine,' she said. 'Oh, forget it. It really doesn't matter.'

Jeanne was frowning. 'But are you sure? Look, for a long time Raoul has said Drew has changed, changed radically. No more of his little flings, no more *petites amies.*'

Had Drew been hiding it from Raoul or was this true? Helen looked at her with uncertainty, biting her lip.

'Raoul and I discussed it. There was some surprise.' Jeanne's eyes held that cynical glint. Although she was kind and warm and friendly, she had a harder attitude to life, she was very much more sophisticated than Helen. 'Well,' she shrugged, 'for a leopard to change his spots does cause surprise and, perhaps, a certain amusement.'

Helen stiffened. 'Amusement?' Her tone was unconsciously cold and Jeanne laughed softly.

'Ah, you don't like that? Well, you know, men like my Raoul admire and envy the freebooting pirates like Drew. They may have opted for a quiet life by the fire, but they still have little yearnings.' Her face grew

sober. 'Once, some years ago, Raoul had more than
little yearnings.'

Helen looked at her in shocked distress.

Jeanne grinned, hardness in the line of her mouth.
'She was very charming, very pretty. Raoul was having
a bad time at work—a tough period for him. And he
felt suddenly old, past it. So,' she spread her hands, 'he
looked around for some magic talisman to make him
young again. A little actress of twenty is some talisman.'

Helen winced. 'I'm sorry, Jeanne.'

'I was too,' said Jeanne. *'Désolée, tu sais.'* Then she
gave Helen a little wink. 'But, I told myself, two can
play at that game. I had my hair re-styled, I bought
some very expensive new clothes, and I went to a few
parties alone. It didn't take Raoul long to wonder what
I was up to, and then to start getting annoyed. You
know, it is one thing for a man to play around and quite
another for him to wonder if his safe, cosy home is
breaking up around his ears. I never mentioned his
little actress to him and he never told me. But he
stopped it overnight and we had a second honeymoon
at Provence without the boys.'

Helen smiled. 'And it worked? You're very clever.'

'He hasn't looked aside since,' Jeanne shrugged. 'He
got a fright and I think he realised he couldn't have his
cake and eat it.'

There was a silence and Helen realised that Jeanne
was watching her expectantly. She smiled. 'It isn't
quite the same thing, Jeanne,' she told her. 'Our situation isn't like that.'

'But something is troubling you? If I can help in any
way . . .'

'You're very kind.'

Jeanne considered her, head to one side. 'You have a most striking face. *Spirituelle*, I think—those huge blue eyes, that lovely blonde hair. Raoul calls you *la petite séductrice de Drew*. I think he feels you have emasculated him.'

Helen's eyes widened, startled.

Jeanne laughed. 'As I said, Raoul feels that Drew had a great life, a roving freebooter, snatching booty at will and never paying for it. Now Drew has joined the other husbands in the pen.'

Was that really how their marriage looked from outside? Helen found the idea so surprising that she could not take it in at all.

But then Raoul would not know what Drew got up to in Africa and the other countries where he came and went like the swallow.

They finished their coffee and rose to leave. Jeanne urged Helen to come to dinner soon. 'Bring Drew. It will eat at Raoul's heart to see Drew faithful at your heels. It makes me laugh to see Raoul grit his teeth every time he remembers Drew's capitulation to the wedding ring!'

Some capitulation, Helen thought drily, as she continued with her shopping. She spent an hour frowning over accessories, trying to match shoes and bags, choosing scarves and gloves.

Drew and Philip had not returned when she arrived back at the apartment. Madame Lefeuvre greeted her eagerly and launched into one of her interminable tales of her feud with the concierge. 'So, *madame*, I asked her: who do you think you are? You know that couple on the second floor, *madame*? The bald-headed one with the *petite poule*? Well, who is to say married or not married? And anyway, is it any business of hers? Reading their letters, *tu sais*? Spying, listening to telephone calls. Is that what they pay her for?'

Helen listened, amused at the ferocity with which Madame pursued the feud. Everything was grist to their mill. They argued over which butcher in the neighbourhood had the best meat, over whether Madame Lefeuvre should feed the pigeons which pattered across the roofs or not, over delays which Madame Lefeuvre claimed were caused by the concierge deliberately holding back the post which was delivered at the desk downstairs.

'But, when I go past her just now, I tap my nose. Nothing more—*rien, tu sais*? Just a little tap.' Her dark eyes glittered. 'She is so angry she almost spits!'

Helen managed to escape at last and went into her own room to gaze along the row of dresses in her fitted wardrobe. One caught her eye and she pulled it out, looked at it doubtfully. She had never worn such a dress before.

She heard Drew's voice speaking in his rattling French to Madame Lefeuvre and then the two men walking past Helen's door on their way to change for dinner. A reckless look came into her face. She would wear the dress she decided.

She took her time in dressing and was just ready when she heard footsteps moving towards the salon. Gathering up her nerve, she opened the door and walked towards the room.

It was Philip, not Drew, who stood pouring himself a drink. He swung with a smile and his eyes widened as he looked at Helen. That quick glance lifted her spirits. She saw the effect on Philip of the daring little black dress and was delighted.

Coughing, a little red, Philip asked: 'Can I pour you a drink, Helen?'

'Thank you,' she smiled, coming over to join him. 'A Martini, thank you.'

'Dry?'

'Please,' she said, and watched him pour the drink.

'Ice?' He held his hands poised over the ice bowl and she nodded. He picked up the tongs and dropped a piece of ice into the drink. Helen took the glass and moved to the couch.

Philip hovered uncertainly, his glass of whisky in his hand. She patted the couch.

'Do sit down, Philip.'

He sat down reluctantly and she smiled at him. 'How long did it take you to make this kit for Stephen?'

He launched into talk of this with relief. She saw that she made him nervous. As he talked his eyes flickered over her and away again. Helen knew why: she had never worn a dress like the one she was wearing now and it gave a new dimension to her appearance. She leaned back, her glass in her hand, watching him, smiling.

'Was the new machinery promising?' she asked when he fell silent.

'It had several original improvements,' he said. 'Drew seemed quite pleased. He hasn't ordered, but I think he may.'

'He values your opinion.'

Philip looked pleased and shy, his brown face filled with shifting emotion. 'I told him I was impressed.'

'When you've finished in Paris, will you be coming

to London? Do come and see Stephen to give him the present yourself. It would delight him to get a visitor from Africa. He'd like you to tell him all about life out there. Drew is thinking of letting us come out and see Kowoli for ourselves—Stephen is eager to see where his daddy works.'

'Would you come?' Philip asked, the deep voice resonant.

'Do you think I'd like it?'

Philip looked down at her and whisked his eyes away. 'I think it would like you. The men would be knocked for six.'

She laughed. 'What a charming compliment!'

Philip had too much integrity to flirt with her, but he couldn't keep his eyes off her and she was aware of it. She was listening for the sound of Drew's steps and waiting with an ache in the pit of her stomach for him to walk into the room. Suddenly she heard his steps. Turning to Philip with a faint smile she said, 'Your tie isn't straight.'

Philip glanced down. Helen put down her glass and swivelled towards him, adjusted his tie carefully, knowing that Drew had walked into the room.

Although it was true that Philip's tie had been clumsily knotted and straggling towards one side of his neck, she had deliberately chosen to make the intimate little gesture of straightening it for him merely to annoy Drew. When she glanced up at Philip with a smile, though, she regretted her act of defiance. Philip was very flushed, his eyes fixed on her in a way which disturbed her.

'Thanks,' he muttered. He glanced past her and said uneasily, 'Whisky, Drew?'

'Yes,' said Drew, strolling forwards. Philip shot off to get the drink and Drew took his place beside Helen. She met his eyes nervously, reading anger in his face. He ran a cool glance over her and she saw his brows lift.

'Very sexy,' he murmured drily.

Philip came back with Drew's whisky and stood, uncomfortably, swirling his own whisky around his glass, averting his eyes from the seductive curves of Helen's body in the black dress. It had been an impulse buy which she had never had the nerve to wear before. She couldn't remember now what had made her buy it in the first place. Perhaps in the boutique it had looked less dynamic. There was little of it, but what there was clung tightly to every curve and suggested the little of her that remained unrevealed.

Philip talked about the machinery he and Drew had seen and Drew answered calmly. 'I think I'll put in an order, but first we must work out the statistics. I'll get the accountants on it. It would have to pay its way or it wouldn't be worth shipping out.'

'How did you get on with your shopping, Helen?'

Drew's question made her start. She glanced at him and found his eyes on the deep plunge of her neckline, probing the revealed white flesh between her breasts.

Flushed, she said, 'I met Jeanne over lunch.'

Drew's eyes rose. 'What's she doing back in Paris? Don't tell me Raoul's been at it again?'

Helen opened her eyes wide. Did Drew know about Raoul's brief affair with an actress? Their glances held and Drew made a wry face.

'Or didn't you know?' he asked coolly.

'Jeanne did mention something,' she admitted

cagily. 'But this time they're both back from Lyons.
Raoul had a board meeting.'

'Ah,' Drew nodded.

'She invited us for dinner.'

'Did you fix a date?'

Helen shook her head and he spread his hands.
'Just as well. I don't intend to stay over here for
long.'

Helen glanced away. 'Are you going back to
Kowoli?'

'I haven't made up my mind,' Drew shrugged. 'I
might come on to London.' He turned back towards
Philip. 'I think you ought to take a little break before
you fly back too, Philip. Heaven knows, you could do
with a holiday. Your people live in Durham, don't
they?'

Philip nodded.

'Why not go up there and relax for a few weeks?
We can spare you.'

'I did think I'd look in at London,' Philip said uncertainly, giving Helen a brief glance.

'Of course you must,' she said at once, knowing
Stephen's construction kit was in his mind. 'In fact I
sent a card to Stephen this morning, promising him
you'd come and see him soon.'

Philip's colour deepened under the tan of his
skin. 'He probably doesn't remember me,' he muttered.

She saw the look in his face and felt a twinge of
pity. 'Of course he does,' she assured him.

Madame Lefeuvre came in to announce dinner and
they all moved into the dining-room. Helen had had
recesses set into the walls to display some exquisite

old China which her father had given her and Drew.
They were pieces too precious to be used except for
very special occasions, their glaze faded, their surfaces
worn down by handling over the years, but they looked
good in their glass cases. Philip looked at them before
he sat down, eyeing them admiringly.

'Your taste is superb, Helen,' he said awkwardly,
seating himself. 'Did you plan the whole of the apartment?'

She nodded. 'Drew gave me a free hand.'

'And a free purse,' Drew commented drily. 'Her
taste is rather expensive.'

'You told me to get the best,' she retorted.

'And you certainly did that,' Drew drawled.

During dinner, Philip kept his eyes on his plate,
talking in his deep voice only if he was directly asked
a question. Helen realised, with some concern, that
he was drinking rather heavily. He had had three
glasses before going in to dinner, each one rather more
than a double, and now he was taking the wine at a surprising speed. His face began to take on aggression, his
eyes over-bright. When Drew talked about the Kowoli
site, Philip argued over some detail, stubbornly stick-
ing to his own view of the matter. Drew quietly
dropped the subject.

After the meal, Drew suggested that they should
take a walk. 'I think we could all do with some fresh
air,' he commented without looking at Philip, who was
now deeply flushed.

In the lift Philip leaned against the wall with his
hands in his pockets and kept his eyes fixed on Helen,
making her nervous. 'Drew,' he said suddenly, 'you're
a lucky fellow.'

Drew's brows were elevated, sardonic amusement in his eyes. 'Thank you.'

'You've got a beautiful wife, lovely wife, and a wonderful son. I envy you, d'you know that?' His voice was thick and deep, slightly uneven. 'You don't deserve them. Don't know how to appreciate them.' The last sentence was so thick it blurred all the words together.

Helen bit her lip. Drew met her worried glance and his face was ironic. He knew that what was bothering her was her own part in Philip's behaviour. She was disgusted with herself, forced to recognise that Philip had drunk deeply because of her.

All evening, he had been looking at her in a way which even Helen could not fail to recognise; admiration, regret, pleasure in his stare. And instead of keeping him icily at a distance, she had been more relaxed with him than she normally was with men. His state was her fault.

When they left the apartment building, the summer night air was warm on Helen's bare arms. Paris was still waking and heated after the long day which had just ended. There were a good many other people walking through the streets, their movements quite different from the way people walked by day. Instead of hurrying with fixed, absorbed faces from place to place, they were drifting, talking, laughing.

Philip fell into step beside Helen, his eyes on her face. 'City of lovers, Paris,' he said.

'Yes,' she agreed slightly dubiously, a faint shiver running over her.

'You cold?' Philip asked, frowning. He touched her arm, his fingers sliding down it caressingly. 'Skin like silk, Helen.' He stopped and started to take off his jacket. 'Mustn't catch cold,' he told her.

Drew jerked the jacket back on to him. 'She isn't cold. Are you, Helen?'

'Not at all,' she said quickly, smiling at Philip. 'It was a kind thought, though. Thank you.'

Drew took her arm in fingers that bit into her and they walked on round a corner. The rhythmic beat of music rose in the night.

'Disco!' said Philip with enthusiasm.

Before they realised it, he had dived down the steps towards a door lit by a flashing neon sign. The music blared as he went inside. Drew gave a grim exclamation, a muttered French oath that made Helen jump. 'You'd better come in with me,' he said angrily. 'I can't leave you out here while I fetch him.' He gave her a look and noted her flinch with saturnine comprehension. 'Yes,' he said softly, 'you deserve a good slap, but I'll deal with you later. Just now, I'm more concerned with finding Philip before he makes a complete idiot of himself.'

She almost covered her ears as they entered the cellar from which the music crashed. It was hard, at first, to see anything but the coloured lights sweeping the crowded room. It was as if the room was being bombarded with virulent lightning and the noise of the band ricocheted from wall to wall, deafening, assaulting. There were dozens of young people packed into the tiny space, moving separately, twisting, swerving, staring at each other.

'Where the hell is he?' Drew said aloud through his teeth, his eyes searching the faces.

He clamped a hand round Helen's wrist and pulled

her down the steps into the crowd. Within a moment
they were separated as the shuffling bodies pulled
them apart. Helen found a hand on her shoulder. 'Hi,'
said a gloomy voice. '*Ça va?*'

She looked in surprise at the young man beside her.
'Excuse me,' she said politely.

'*Anglaise,*' he muttered. 'Hey, chick,' and he grinned
at her, 'dance with me.'

Baffled, she looked round for Drew and could see
nothing of him. The young man laughed. '*Comme ça,*'
he told her, demonstrating.

She could not move either way now, fenced in helplessly. She found herself squashed against the young
man, staring dumbly at his thick mop of tousled hair
which looked as if he had not washed it for months.

He had hot, insolent eyes as he stared at her from
head to toe. More than ever, Helen regretted having
put on the daring little dress. She felt the young
man's hands descend on to her hips. '*En marche,
bébé,*' he growled.

Helen was frightened. The crush of bodies, the
sweep of the strobe lighting, the appalling crash of the
music, hemmed her in against this dreadful young
man, made her tremble with nerves and panic. She put
her hands on the young man's chest and tried to push
him away.

He was not much taller than her, but his orange
T-shirt covered a muscular body and her little push
made no effect on him except to make him laugh. He
bent his face towards her, smiling broadly. '*Em-
brasse-moi, bébé.*' She gasped in shock as the rough-
ness of his mouth forced her own open, her hands
wriggling helplessly, squashed between their bodies.

She was disgusted by the intimacy he was forcing on her, the crude exploration of his hands on her as he kissed her. Bringing her teeth together sharply, she bit him and felt his head jerk back.

'*Sale petite garce!*' he bellowed, looking furious.

At that moment people around them were flung apart and Drew forced a path through to her, his face alien to Helen as without looking at her he went for the young man's throat. She shook in horror, watching the mop of hair as it was shaken violently, the young man swearing thickly in a hoarse voice. Then Drew flung him aside, grabbed Helen's wrist and dragged her from the cellar among babble and waved fists.

Outside Philip was waiting, looking deflated and unhappy. 'You stupid bastard,' Drew barked at him. 'Why the hell did you go in there?'

'Sorry,' Philip mumbled.

Drew looked darkly at Helen, his face torn by rage, then he turned on his heels and strode off, pulling her after him, her wrist held in his steely fingers, so tightly that she felt the blood had been cut off. He walked so fast she had to totter on her tiny high heels to keep up with him, but when she wailed a protest he ignored it, merely giving her a look which promised vengeance as soon as he had her to himself.

She had wanted to see him lose his cool, she thought miserably. Well, she had had her wish! For a second in that crowded, noisy cellar she had seen homicidal rage in Drew's face. She had thought he was going to kill the young man in the orange T-shirt.

Drew had regained his self-control within seconds, but Helen had discovered in those seconds that Drew was dangerous, very dangerous. The mocking grey eyes could be murderous and the handsome, sensual face could tighten into bitter lines.

She ran along behind him like a runaway squaw recaptured by her brave, aware of people's surprised, amused stares as Drew dragged her after him. Philip was hurrying along, too. He caught up with Drew and she heard his anxious voice saying: 'It's my fault, Drew. Don't get angry with Helen.'

'Shut up!' Drew bit out, not slackening his pace an inch.

They regained the entrance to the apartment block and Drew almost threw Helen into the lift. She fell against the steel wall and Philip looked at Drew angrily.

'That's enough,' he said, his voice thick.

The doors closed and the lift began to move smoothly upwards. Drew stood with his back to them both for a few seconds, then he turned and looked at Philip levelly. 'Mind your own business, Philip.'

The tone warned, soft though it was, and Philip tensed belligerently. 'I don't like seeing women pushed around.'

'Leave it,' said Drew, almost bored, his face a stiff mask.

'Now look——' Philip began, and Drew turned his black head to look at him with his lips curling back from his white teeth and rage in his grey eyes.

'You're asking to get your face pushed through the back of your head,' he told him tightly.

Philip stiffened and Helen put a hand on his arm.

'Don't, please,' she said in a shaky voice.

Both men looked at her, but she kept her eyes on Philip. 'Drew's right, Philip. Please, just leave it.'

Philip bowed his head without speaking.

The lift stopped, the doors opened and Drew stood back to let her walk past him to the apartment. She went straight to her room, but Drew was on her heels and when she tried to close her bedroom door he kicked it open, sending her flying across the room. He slammed it and locked it.

Helen stood with her hands clenched at her sides, terrified. Drew stared at her with his back against the door. Without a word he began to loosen his tie.

CHAPTER SIX

SHE swallowed, appalled by the expression on his face. 'I'm sorry!'

'A little late for that,' Drew said savagely. 'You asked for everything that happened. You caused the whole thing—I warned you to leave Philip alone.' He stared down into her face. 'My God, you aren't blind. You must know the poor devil's gone half crazy over you.'

Red washed up her face. She turned away and Drew's hands fell on her shoulders, twisted her back round to face him, staring into her eyes. She felt him searching for reaction, probing to discover exactly how she felt about what he had just said.

'How do you feel about that?'

She didn't answer, her eyes fixed on the floor. Drew shook her roughly, his fingers biting into her. 'Answer! How does it make you feel to know he cares for you? You've knocked him for six.'

'He barely knows me,' she protested.

Drew's mouth twisted bitterly. 'That's the beauty of it. He looks at you and sees a vision of sweetness— big blue eyes, a gentle smile. My God, you've sent him reeling! Even if Philip doesn't know it yet, he's wide open to another disastrous mistake, because you wouldn't be any improvement on his wife. You'd probably do even more damage than she did.'

Helen swung away, putting her hands over her ears.

'I don't want to hear. Don't talk about it!'

Drew took three strides and yanked her hands down, then grabbed her arms and shook her, his face bending over her, his eyes glittering. 'You don't want to hear because that frigid little heart of yours can't take too much real life, can it? You said you knew Philip was vulnerable. What did you mean if not that you realised how he felt?'

She shook her head, distressed. 'I thought ... he was hurt, by his marriage, his wife's death.'

'Oh, that too,' Drew bit out. 'He's had a rough deal, and you've just made it rougher. You must have seen the way he looked at you tonight. He could hardly keep his hands off you. I've known Philip for years, and I've never seen him deliberately get drunk before.'

Helen's face was burning, her eyes pained. 'I'm sorry. I wouldn't have ...' She broke off, biting her lip.

'Wouldn't you?' Drew's eyes flicked over the low-necked dress. 'What was all this in aid of? Why the flaunting little dress?'

She looked away nervously. 'Please ...'

'And you got more than you expected, didn't you? If I hadn't got there God knows what that lout would have done to you.'

She shivered, her lips trembling. 'It was a horrible experience.'

'All experience is horrible to you,' Drew muttered. His lids dropped, hiding his eyes. 'What did you expect? Wearing that dress you were an open invitation.' His voice had slowed, thickened. 'And, my God, you're going to give tonight, Helen!'

Her breath caught. Huskily, she muttered, 'No, Drew!'

She tried to draw away, but he held her with one forceful hand around her upper arm. She struggled, pulling away, but was held helpless. His other hand manipulated her zip. She heard it slide and then the little dress slid away from her. She tried to grasp it, pull it back up, but Drew pushed her hands away, dragging her back against him as the dress rustled to her feet.

'A delightful garment, but I prefer you without it,' he muttered, his eyes moving over her. 'I liked you the way you looked first thing this morning.'

Her frightened eyes rose to his hard face. He slid the straps of her lacy black slip down over her shoulders and ran his lips along the collarbone.

'Don't!' she begged, shivering.

He kissed her throat carefully. She felt the silken brush of her slip as it fell away from her and her heart began to pound feverishly against her ribs.

Drew moved slightly, staring at her slender pale body in the tiny black briefs and bra. His hand went to his shirt. Shaking, she watched him slowly undo it and then discard his jacket.

It joined her clothes on the floor and was followed by his shirt. When Drew's hand moved down to his trousers she gasped and began to fight in earnest, pushing at him, wriggling like an eel in his grip.

He pulled her round, both hands holding her wrists. The hard, sensual face glared down at her. 'I'm taking you, whether you want it or not,' he muttered. 'Fight and I'll hurt you. I warned you, Helen. I told you I'd teach you to be frightened of me.'

'I won't do it again,' she promised hurriedly in the voice of a terrified child.

'You won't,' Drew agreed. 'Tomorrow I'm sending Philip back to Kowoli.' He paused, his face merciless, the long mouth sensual yet set in cruel lines. 'But tonight you're going to pay.'

'Don't, please!' she begged weakly, shivering, although the night air was warm in the quiet room.

Drew's eyes glittered down at her, then he pulled her body towards him and his mouth took savage possession of hers, parting her lips and invading her mouth in a way she had never imagined any man would ever kiss her. Her head fell back. She moaned, stifled, helpless. His hands were moving everywhere, touching her hungrily, fondling, a heat in their movements, a naked desire which mounted to her head and left her trembling in his arms.

His hands lifted her, his kiss still consuming her, and he carried her to the bed. She was so dazed she did not move as he finished stripping. When he slid down on to the bed beside her, she opened her eyes and looked at him almost blankly, shocked to the depths of her whole nature.

She could not remember ever having seen him naked. The night he had forced her it had been dark and she had been too shattered to notice anything about him. Now she saw him and her mouth went dry.

The broad shoulders had a magnificent silky bronze sheen to them, the deep chest as highly tanned by the African sun but roughened by the dark hair which grew down the centre of it. Her eyes flickered and hurriedly moved away.

Drew pushed one hand beneath her back, the other arm going over her body to trap her on the bed. She felt the fastening of her bra unclip and then Drew removed it and threw it over his shoulder.

His hand smoothly ran down her and she gave a stifled little moan, trying to wriggle away.

'You have a beautiful body, Helen,' Drew said suddenly, his voice thickened. He bent his black head until his lips touched the smooth slope of her breast. 'Ah, *dieu, chérie, j'ai envie de toi, laisse-moi t'aimer ce soir.*'

Her numbed mind could not translate the French for a moment. When she did she felt the colour flaring into her face. He wanted her, he had said, and he wanted to make love to her tonight. Although he had threatened her so violently before, there had been a ring of pleading in his tone.

He seemed to be waiting for a reply, his lips teasing the stiff nipples, caressing them delicately so that they hardened even more, and his hand had wandered down the silken curve of her hip and was stroking her thigh, his own thigh moving restlessly against her, his breathing faster and harder as he touched her.

He looked up and she couldn't move or speak, her eyes enormous in her flushed face. He watched her, she thought, like a cat, with eyes that gleamed in the dark, a cat which has trapped its prey and is waiting triumphantly to devour it but enjoying the anguished beating of its heart, the shaking of the body as it waits to be devoured.

He closed his eyes. His face was pale suddenly. He began muttering in French again and she strained to hear, not understanding the husky words. '*J'ai attendu cela des années, des années de frustration.'*

'What?' she asked anxiously.

He opened his eyes and gave her a strange, fixed look. 'Years,' he said. 'Years of wanting you. I might just as well have sat and hungered for the moon. You've been deaf, dumb and blind to the human race for most of your life, but tonight you're coming down off that star, Helen, if I have to half kill you to get you.'

She gave a cry of wild panic as he moved. He took her violently because her body was threshing in strained fear as he forced her back on to the pillows. Her hands and feet were icy cold and her teeth chattered. Drew's face was darkly angry as he stared at her. 'Don't tremble like that,' he grated.

'I can't help it,' she whispered threadily.

'Shock,' he said bitterly. 'My God! Does it horrify you so much?'

She felt his body clench, his intake of breath and knew he was going to leave her. Her arms went round his neck, clinging.

'Drew,' she said, not knowing how else to tell him, afraid even to phrase it in her own mind.

Drew understood, though. With a swift look into her eyes he bent his head to take her mouth again. As he fiercely continued, the coldness left her and heat took its place. She arched towards him, her hands digging into his shoulders, aware of his tense excitement, listening to the heavy beat of his heart and aroused by the feelings she found in him.

At last she admitted that she wanted him, heedless of what triumph it would give him to hear her wild cries, and when his husky voice groaned thickly in her ear she did not even try to decipher the muttered words or ask herself whether he even knew who she was, or felt anything but a sensual enjoyment in the act itself. It no longer mattered. Drew might be using her body because she had denied it so long. He might be merely a man who liked making love to women, and did not much care which one he took to bed. But to-night she knew the intolerable pressure of a drive for satisfaction so intense that when it came she almost lost consciousness, her nails tearing his shoulders, her body pulsing in a consummation which was almost agonising.

Afterwards she lay and felt him in every pore of her body. He had imprinted himself upon her, swam in her bloodstream, breathed in her lungs, was absorbed into the cellular structure of her skin.

Drew, she thought dazedly. Drew. The silence between them was thick with unspoken words.

'Go to sleep, Helen,' Drew said at last, his voice drained. 'The sweetest sleep in the world comes now.'

It did, she found. She fell asleep almost at once and slept deeply, but all night she was subconsciously aware of the warm male pressure against her, the heavy weight of his arm across her body, the breathing beside her in the night.

In the morning she remembered almost as soon as she had woken up and her lashes flicked open, but the bed was empty beside her. Drew had gone.

It was just before eleven when she went into the dining-room. Madame Lefeuvre gave her the coy little smile which she had worn ever since Helen and Drew arrived together, arousing her romantic notions of their relationship. 'Bonjour, madame. You slept well, eh?'

'Very well,' Helen said shyly, particularly embarrassed because for once Madame was quite right in her suspicions.

Madame's smile broadened. 'Monsieur, you see, he told me to leave you to sleep for as long as you wished. Do not disturb her, he said. So,' she shrugged in her Gallic way, her plump shoulders expressive, 'I let you sleep. I will make fresh coffee for you now.'

As she walked to the door, Helen said with as much coolness as she could muster, 'My husband has gone out with Mr Cameron?'

Madame Lefeuvre halted, smiling widely. 'Monsieur Cameron, he has left, taken his luggage and gone. To the airport, one supposes. He rang them very early this morning.'

Helen paled. Drew had kept his word, then. He was sending Philip back to Kowoli. Helen felt bitterly ashamed of her behaviour last night. She had ruined poor Philip's first holiday for months.

Madame went on softly, 'And as for Monsieur ton mari, he will be out all day. He told me he would be back late. No dinner for him tonight. He said you were dining out yourself.'

Helen looked at her blankly, then pulled herself together. 'Oh, yes,' she said. 'Yes, I'd forgotten.' What on earth did Drew mean? Dining out?

She lingered over her coffee, trying to make sense of it. Drew had gone out—that surprised her after last night. She had somehow expected him to want to see her this morning. Why had he gone like that, without a word?

A sparrow was chirping on the wide windowsill beyond the draped curtains. She watched it, a numbed feeling creeping over her.

Had last night meant anything at all to Drew? The revelation to her of how explosive her own reaction could be had masked from her what Drew was feeling. He had told her nothing. His muttered words had been in thick French, indecipherable to her last night. The whirlwind of passion might have been novel and shattering to her, but what it had been to him she could not even guess. He was used to such scenes, perhaps. Had it all been a familiar story to him? A reluctant woman forced to submit and then to give eagerly without reserve?

She closed her eyes, white to her lips. She had gone crazy last night. This morning she felt sick.

Drew had walked away without looking back. He had got all he wanted from her and now he was hunting elsewhere for fresh prey.

She had been warned. Why on earth had she let herself fall a victim to that practised male charm, that sex appeal which she had resisted for so long?

She got up abruptly. She was not sitting around here waiting for him like a lovesick idiot. She wasn't going to have him guess what he had done to her last night.

She rang the airport and booked a flight to London at three o'clock, then went into her room to pack her clothes. As she came out of the room Madame Lefeuvre stared at her in disbelief. *'Que passe, madame?'*

'I have to return to London at once,' Helen said coolly, her face returned to normal during her time in the bedroom. 'My taxi should be here soon. You'll explain to my husband that I've been called away?'

The housekeeper looked horrified. '*Mais, madame* ...'

There was a ring at the door. 'Ah, there's the taxi,' Helen said hurriedly.

Madame Lefeuvre pursued her to the lift, the taxi driver carrying the cases, and begged her to leave a written message for Drew.

'He'll understand,' Helen said with conscious irony.

'But I must give him some idea,' Madame protested unhappily.

Helen paused, a dry smile on her face. 'Tell him I have to go back, that's all,' she shrugged, getting into the lift.

The taxi took a long time to get to the airport. Helen had a grinding feeling of anxiety all the time they were on the way. She was desperate to get that plane, to get away before Drew could catch up with her. He might get back to the apartment and discover her flight and then he might be annoyed enough to come after her. Once she was in London, she would feel safer.

She arrived with just a few moments to spare before the flight was closed. She was hustled on board, out of breath, and began to move along the plane with her flight bag in her hand.

'Helen!'

The astonished voice brought her head round and she stared down at Philip incredulously. 'What are you doing on this flight?'

'I'm on my way to London,' he said. 'Didn't Drew tell you?'

Her face froze up. 'I haven't seen him,' she said. Her eye caught that of the large, bald man seated beside Philip and the man gave them both a little smile.

He rose, bowing. 'Please, take my seat.'

'Oh, no, I couldn't,' she began to protest, but he was already collecting his bag and newspapers and was moving off to take the free seat reserved for her.

'Thank you,' she said to his departing back, and he turned to smile admiringly at her.

Sinking into the seat beside Philip she settled herself without looking at him for a few moments. The lights flashed on and she strapped herself into her seat. The captain's voice droned overhead and Helen glanced at Philip sideways. He looked as pale and drawn as she felt. He had a grim look about his mouth and eyes this morning. Catching her glance, he looked at her directly.

'I apologise for last night,' he muttered below his breath.

'It doesn't matter,' she said at once.

'It was a disgusting exhibition,' he went on huskily. 'Drew really pulled my ears for it this morning, and he's right. I should have known better. I'm very sorry I got you into that ghastly dive.'

'No harm done,' she said too brightly, flushing.

He gave her a brief look. 'When I saw you with that swine mauling you about I could have killed him myself. I was coming over to do just that when Drew shoved me out of the way. He was hopping mad, wasn't he? I've seen Drew like that once before. There was some trouble on site and Drew flared up like burn-

ing oil. He keeps it down most of the time, of course.
His self-control is phenomenal.'

'Yes,' she said drily.

'Last night I thought he might kill that oaf, though.
His face was manic.'

'Yes,' she whispered, bending her head. Manic, she
thought. She remembered Drew's taut, dark features,
the murderous grey eyes, and shivered.

'All my fault, the whole thing,' Philip said miserably.
'I suppose coming back to Europe sparked it all off—
I met my wife on a visit back home.'

She sighed. 'I am sorry about her, Philip.'

'We were all washed up, anyway. That made it
worse, somehow. It made me feel a real swine.'

'You mustn't,' she protested.

'Can't help it,' he muttered. 'You see, taking her
out to Kowoli wasn't such a great idea. She was bored
and I was working hard all the time. She got left on
her own a lot—too much. Drew told me to knock
it off a bit, warned me I was running a risk with all
that overtime, but I suppose I was just dim. It never
entered my head that she'd look elsewhere.'

The words were spilling out of him hurriedly, as
though he was dying to tell someone, to talk about it.
She couldn't refuse to listen. Philip quite obviously
needed to talk.

His face was pale and sweating, his eyes on his
hands. 'There were plenty of men ready to keep her
amused, but I was too blind to realise what was going
on for a long time. None of my friends liked to tell me,
I suppose. There's a club there for the men, and she
used to go almost every night. There was a succession
of them, I never did find out just how many and who,

I preferred not to know. I might have felt I had to do something about it, and I could hardly blame them for taking what was on offer.'

Helen winced, turning her head away. Philip caught the little movement and his eyes fixed on her averted profile.

'She wasn't anything like you,' he said huskily. 'Drew's always away, but you've never looked at another man, have you?'

Her eyes widened and her skin whitened. She didn't answer, her face shaken. Philip was blind to her real situation, seeing in her mockery of a marriage all the admirable fidelity of a wife who would never be tempted.

'I realised how lucky Drew was when I came over to London that time. He's not only got you but he's got little Stephen. Drew has a real family. I don't blame him for keeping you in London. If you were mine, I'd lock you up and throw away the key.'

She looked at him then, almost miserably. 'Don't put me on a pedestal, Philip. I'm not some sort of angel.'

He put his hand over her twisting fingers. 'You look as if you're going to cry,' he said deeply. 'Don't. I should never have mentioned the damned miserable business to you at all. Drew would half kill me if he knew.'

'Your wife was only human, Philip,' she whispered. 'She may have behaved badly, but maybe she was miserable herself.'

He grimaced. 'So she said, but nothing could excuse the things she got up to—you wouldn't begin to understand, Helen.'

Her face creased in a frown. She didn't understand, it was true. Married to a kind, sensitive man like Philip, how could his wife have been such a fool?

'Perhaps she was trying to make you jealous?' she suggested.

His eyes flicked at her wryly. 'Forget it, Helen. As I say, you come from another planet. You couldn't understand. I wish I didn't have to remember it all. It's like a sick dream, something you wish you could forget but can't.'

'You need a holiday,' she said anxiously.

He nodded, removing his hands.

For a while they were both silent, then Philip said: 'But why are you going back to London so soon? I thought you and Drew were staying over there for a while.'

'Drew is,' she said. 'I have to get back.' Hurriedly thinking, she added, 'My agency business needs attention. Did you know I helped run a business?' She began to tell him about it and he said with a smile,

'Of course, I know Janet and her husband. He's always boasting about her business acumen.'

'He's quite right. Janet has a good brain. We started our agency mostly to give her work herself, but now she's needed full-time to run the place and we employ quite a number of women.'

'How do you manage to pack so much into your life?' Philip asked admiringly. 'The little boy, your music, your homes and a business career too!'

'Oh, I do very little about the agency. Janet is the lynchpin of that organisation. I just put up the money and do the odd day here and there when she needs a break.'

'All the same, you certainly keep yourself busy. I suppose you must miss Drew badly while he's away.'

Helen smiled politely and didn't answer that. The drinks trolley arrived and she accepted a glass of gin and tonic while Philip had a whisky. They sipped their drinks and stared at nothing, then Helen pretended to feel sleepy and lay back with her eyes closed. She felt Philip's eyes on her from time to time and wished she could be less conscious of the way he looked at her. Drew had made her aware of it when she might otherwise have been less self-conscious.

Philip was eager to find something to replace his wife, to heal the scars left by that experience. She hoped he would soon forget her and find someone else, someone who would give him the love he needed.

When his eyes were on her, Helen was more and more aware that Philip did not see her at all, only a dream he was carrying around like a faded photograph. He imagined her as the loving, faithful wife he yearned for and had not achieved. She was certainly nothing like his dead wife, Helen thought wryly, but for very different reasons from the ones which Philip attributed to her. She had never betrayed Drew because no man had ever attracted her, but would Philip want a wife like her, if she was available? Would he want a marriage like the one she had with Drew? He saw it through rosy glasses, imagining them as the perfect lovers, and even though he was, she realised now, slightly jealous of Drew, he still liked to believe that Helen was some sort of perfect woman.

She couldn't explain to him how false his views were without betraying herself, Drew, her marriage, even though she found it in some way painful to know that

Philip had put her on that pedestal of his and was wor-
shipping her wrongly without knowing anything about
her.

At Heathrow, Philip managed to find a taxi to drive
them both into London and as they drove she invited
him to have dinner with her that evening. 'You can
have a chat with Stephen before he goes to bed, then,'
she told him.

Philip gave her a faintly anxious look. 'You don't
think Drew would mind?'

For a moment she almost said: Drew isn't here,
and then she saw just how dangerous that remark
could sound, so instead she said quietly, 'Of course
he won't mind, Philip. Why on earth should he?'

She knew, in fact, that Drew would mind. He would
be furious if he knew. But she didn't care. Drew had
walked out on her after last night and she would like
to kill him.

Philip grimaced. 'No, of course not.' He laughed
with a certain self-derision. 'Drew wouldn't feel he
had anything to worry about where I was concerned.'

She did not answer that because either way she
could cause trouble if she gave any reply.

When they reached her home she took Philip straight
up to see Stephen, who greeted them with wild enthusiasm. 'Mummy! Mummy! I didn't know you
were coming back today!' He clambered into her
arms as she bent towards him and she lifted him to
kiss his flushed little face.

Over her shoulder Stephen eyed Philip with interest. 'Hallo,' Philip said. 'You've grown a lot. I didn't
recognise you for a minute.'

'I recognised you,' Stephen said proudly, and Philip's

face lit up. 'You gave me Gerry.' He turned his head to wave at where the giraffe sat among his gang of toys—the battered old teddy Drew had given him, in its striped football jersey, the long red racing car which Grey had bought him for Christmas and several of his other favourite toys. Stephen had an orderly mind. He liked to arrange his possessions around him. He was possessive, tenacious, a boy who knew his own mind and had a strong will.

Philip picked up the giraffe and pulled its tail to make the head nod. 'I brought you something else this time,' he said shyly. He had a large parcel in his flight bag and produced it now, offering it to Stephen with a little grin.

Stephen eagerly unwrapped it and exclaimed in delight over the contents. 'Uncle Philip made them himself, darling,' Helen told him.

Stephen looked impressed. 'Did you really? How?'

Helen left them alone, smiling as she heard them talking about the way Philip had made the kit, the tools he had used, the time it had taken.

She went up later to remove Philip and he went ahead after a regretful parting from Stephen while Helen kissed her son goodnight. 'I'm going to build roads like my daddy,' Stephen said belligerently, staring at her. 'Where is my daddy?'

'In Paris, darling,' she said with a quick look at his square-cut little face. His eyes looked remarkably like Drew's hard eyes as he stared at her.

'When's my daddy coming home? Why can't we go and live in Africa with him and build roads? I could learn to build them then.'

She swallowed. 'Maybe we will, one day.'

'I want to go now. Uncle Philip said my daddy was with you in Paris. Why couldn't I go and see my daddy? Why did you leave me at home?'

Helen did not know what to answer. Her face disturbed she said gently, 'I didn't know Daddy was going to be in Paris, Stephen, or I would certainly have taken you. It was a last-minute change of plan.'

Stephen kept his eyes on her, his face flushed and aggressive. 'Olivia Wrighton says her mummy is going to divorce her daddy and that means he's going to go away and not come back, and Olivia says she's glad because he shouts, but I don't want you to divorce my daddy.'

Helen stared, suddenly guessing that this was what had been worrying him lately. 'When did Olivia tell you that?' she asked softly.

'Ages ago,' Stephen said flatly. 'She says her mummy is going to get a new daddy that doesn't shout, but I don't want a new daddy. I want my own daddy.'

'I promise you I'm not going to divorce your daddy,' Helen said clearly, holding his eyes. 'I never would, Stephen, and as soon as he can, he's going to fly home to see you and maybe take you out to Kowoli for a visit. He told me he spoke to you on the phone and you said you wanted him to come home.'

Stephen relaxed, his small limbs draining of the tension which had held them. 'Well,' he said thoughtfully, 'that's all right. Will he let me build roads with him?'

'You must ask him,' said Helen, kissing him.

His arms came up to hug her and he said into her slender shoulder, 'Uncle James is ugly.'

Helen stifled a little giggle. 'You shouldn't make remarks about grown-ups, Stephen.'

'And,' Stephen added in a soft voice, 'Daddy is bigger.'

'Much bigger,' Helen agreed, still smiling helplessly.

'When I'm ten I shall be as big as Daddy.'

'Well, almost,' she compromised.

'I'll have a motorbike and I'll build roads.' Stephen yawned, ready for sleep and contented now that he had got the answer he wanted from her. 'And I'll ride right over Uncle James.'

Helen retreated before laughter overcame her and had to struggle with a desire to tell Philip what Stephen had said, but Philip would merely be horrified. Only Drew would appreciate what their son had said about poor James.

Obviously, Stephen had viewed James's visits with alarm and foreboding after Olivia's story about her own parents being divorced. It was amazing what children talked about, she thought, and how much they knew of what was happening in the adult world around them. She knew that the Wrightons were getting a divorce. Olivia went to the same play-school as Stephen, a pretty little girl with long straight hair and a wistful face. It was saddening to think of her burdened with such adult problems, but there had been trouble in that household for a long time, Helen was aware. George Wrighton had a violent temper and his wife was unable to stop herself from baiting it. The two of them quarrelled like cat and dog, no atmosphere in which to bring up a child.

She wished Stephen had thought of mentioning it to her before. Why had he chosen to talk to Drew about it? Had he asked Drew if there was a divorce in the offing in their own family? She wondered if Stephen had mentioned to Drew her own planned trip to Paris, and if that had been what brought Drew to Paris himself, to see if he could find out how much fire there was in Stephen's smoke about James Farrier.

She stood on the spacious landing, breathing in the fragrance of a bowl of white lilac on a table beside her. Had Drew deliberately seduced her in order to make sure their marriage held together? He had married her just to get his hands on her father's company and if they were divorced he might well lose control of it. Grey more and more relinquished control to Drew, she knew. Her father was an adoring grandfather and so proud of Stephen that he was deeply grateful to Drew for giving him the boy.

Was that Drew's motive in forcing her to sleep with him last night?

CHAPTER SEVEN

SHE was about to join Philip in the drawing-room when her parents arrived, looking at her incredulously as they came into the hall. 'What are you doing back?' Leona asked her with raised eyebrows. 'I thought you were in Paris for another two days.'

'I finished my shopping early,' she lied, kissing her mother lightly on her cheek, careful not to meet her eyes.

Grey said jovially, 'Stephen in bed, is he? We came over to make sure he was all right.'

'He's fine. I've just said goodnight to him. Why not go up before he falls asleep? Nanny will have got him into bed by now.'

'Might as well,' said Grey with a pretence of reluctance, moving eagerly to the stairs. Since Stephen's birth he had become totally absorbed in his grandson, spending every spare moment he could with him.

Leona said coolly, 'I'll let him see Stephen on his own. He prefers that.'

It was true, but it was also true that Leona was by no means as devoted a grandparent as Grey. She was pleased to have a grandson, but she had too much in her life that interested her more. She looked at Helen now, her blue eyes flicking over her, the pale lavender rinse of her hair making her look oddly like the fairy on a Christmas tree.

'What did you get in Paris? Anything special?' The

only ground on which they ever met was the subject of clothes.

'A number of things from Solange—her collection is rather good this year, I thought.'

'Got them with you?' Leona automatically fiddled with her hair, a movement demonstrating her usual boredom in Helen's presence.

'No, they'll be arriving later.'

'How was Paris?' Leona half-yawned, glancing at herself in the hall mirror, inspecting the faint lines around her eyes with a discontented twist of her mouth. From a distance she still managed to look around thirty. It was only at close quarters that one saw the dissolving touch of age on skin and muscle, the faint wrinkling here and there, the sag of the throat.

'Busy,' said Helen, wishing she could make some sort of contact with her yet knowing it was hopeless. 'I've got a guest for dinner, by the way.'

Leona did not expect much of Helen's guests. 'Janet, I suppose?' she asked with a grimace.

'A friend of Drew's—Philip Cameron.'

The dark painted brows lifted. 'Does Drew know he's here?' Slyness came into Leona's face.

Helen gave her a dry look and opened the door without answering. Philip rose as they came into the room and looked at Leona politely. Helen murmured an introduction and Leona swam forward, her whole manner altering, as it always did in the presence of a man.

She eyed his height, the width of his shoulders and his tan with an interested gaze. 'Hallo,' she said huskily, and Philip's eyes flickered with a dismay which made Helen want to laugh or cry.

He offered his hand and Leona deliberately left her

fingers in it, smiling at him. Philip moved back after a moment, flushed. Leona turned to her daughter. 'As you're back we might as well dine with you, but I suppose you'd better clear it with Mrs Creel.'

There was faint sarcasm in that. Helen said politely, 'Of course. I'll speak to her.' She left the room, knowing that Leona wanted her to leave her alone with Philip, embarrassed by her mother's blatant interest in him. Shrugging, she thought: well, Philip is old enough to look after himself.

Mrs Creel took on a sulky air when Helen asked her to stretch the arranged meal to accommodate four. 'It's short notice, madam. I don't know if I can.'

'Please, Mrs Creel,' Helen said softly, smiling at her. 'I would be grateful. I know it makes things difficult, but I'm sure you'll cope.'

There was dislike between Mrs Creel and Leona, largely based on Leona's high-handed interference in the running of the house whenever it crossed her mind. Mrs Creel was not, of course, unaware of the coolness between Helen and her mother, and she openly tried to side with Helen, although Helen did not encourage her.

'I'm afraid it's vichyssoise, Mrs Lincoln,' Mrs Creel observed with satisfaction, 'which your mother doesn't like.' And Helen guessed that if it hadn't been, it would be now that Leona was going to be eating it.

'You'd better offer an alternative my mother does like, then,' Helen told her gently as she left the kitchen.

When she rejoined them, Philip had a hunted air and Leona was purring with amusement. They were on the couch, the polished talons of Leona's curved nails on his sleeve, and Philip was very flushed. He was not

used to predatory women and did not know how to deal
with her. He threw Helen a pleading look as she entered.

Grey came down a moment later, smiling. 'He's
asleep,' he informed her. 'Went off like a light.'

'Thank you for coming in to see him,' Helen told
him, noting that Leona had relaxed her pursuit of
Philip under her husband's eyes. Their marriage had
been almost entirely empty, Helen knew, but they did
keep up appearances and Leona knew better than to
flirt with other men in front of Grey.

Her mother's eyes sharpened furiously as she viewed
the soup. 'Leek and potato soup!'

'Vichyssoise, madam,' Mrs Creel said smugly.

'What else is there?' Helen asked quietly, her eyes
on Mrs Creel.

Sulkily, the housekeeper said: 'Smoked mackerel,
madam.'

'Isn't there melon or grapefruit?' Leona demanded.
'I don't like mackerel.'

'Good stuff, this soup,' Grey said as he tasted it.
'That woman can certainly cook!'

'You like the vile stuff,' Leona muttered discontent-
edly.

'Try the mackerel,' Grey advised, and she looked at
him with rage. He never did take any notice of her
likes and dislikes.

Glancing at his daughter, Grey said cheerfully,
'Stephen seems brighter tonight, far more lively.
Seemed a bit off colour to me the last day or so. Missed
you, I expect.' He gave her a look which was surprising
to her, a slow thoughtful look, moving over her cool
elegant figure in the delicate green dress she wore, from

her coiled hair to her slender hands. 'Very fond of you, Stephen.'

Helen felt herself flush slightly. Philip looked across the table at her with something of the same expression.

'I'm sure he is,' he said deeply.

Helen bent over her soup.

Leona looked in disbelief at the food Mrs Creel began to ladle on to her plate later. 'Coq au vin, madam,' Mrs Creel said with an unctuous smile.

Leona gave her a look which could have killed. 'You know very well I don't like chicken. It brings me out in a rash.'

Making an amazed face, Mrs Creel said, 'Not chicken, madam. That would be strawberries.'

'Chicken,' Leona said through her teeth, her lacquered face glittering with rage. 'Especially in red wine which is as acid as this from the look of it, and mushrooms too ... my God! I'd never sleep. Is there any salad?'

Mrs Creel looked delightedly at her. 'Not a leaf of lettuce, madam.'

Helen met her eyes across the table. 'Bring my mother a plain omelette, Mrs Creel, when you've served the rest of us.'

Mrs Creel closed her lips on whatever she had been about to say. Moving away from Leona, she muttered, 'Yes, madam.'

Helen rarely used that cool, clear tone, but when she did Mrs Creel knew better than to argue. There was silence as she finished serving the meal before sliding out of the room.

'Really, Helen!' Leona burst out.

'I'm sorry, Leona,' said Helen. 'I'm sure the omelette will be delicious, though, and you do like omelettes.'

Leona subsided, silently fuming, sitting there like a dormant volcano with her cheeks reddened with rage, not rouge. Philip, with what Helen recognised as real self-sacrifice, turned to smile at Leona and say, 'I haven't been in London for ages. It seems changed, somehow. Bigger, noisier.'

Leona was diverted, as he intended, and launched into a monologue on the subject of London's changing face. Having a male audience always cheered her and she forgot her fury with Mrs Creel, especially when the promised omelette turned out to be exceptionally moist and fluffy.

Fortunately she was able to view the orange sorbet with some acceptance too, and so the meal ended on quite a high note, with her giggling with Philip over some complicated anecdote of marital trouble among her friends. That Philip found this painful and distasteful clearly escaped her. Leona had a cynical disrespect for marriage which she did not trouble to hide from him and Philip looked at her with cold eyes as he listened.

After dinner, Philip asked Helen to play to them and her parents looked bored but did not protest. As she played a Mozart rondo her father's snores rose above the sound of the piano and she turned her head to smile at Philip, who was looking shocked. Leona was viewing her nail varnish with fascination, her mouth wry.

'Oh, come along, Grey,' she said irritably when Helen had come to a stop and Grey launched himself heavily to his feet, saying to Helen with a grimace,

'Sorry about that. Tired, I'm afraid—too much good food.'

'Not here, you didn't,' Leona snapped, dragging him off. 'That woman can't cook for toffee!'

Helen went to see them out, kissing the cheek her mother turned to her in a bored way and smiling at her father. 'Thank you for calling in to check on Stephen. I like to think you're looking after him when I'm not here.'

'Any time, any time,' Grey said honestly. 'My pleasure.'

She closed the front door on them and walked back into the room. Philip was on his feet. 'I'd better be off too,' he said. 'I very much enjoyed the music, Helen. Thank you.'

She wanted to apologise for her mother and knew she couldn't, so she just smiled at him warmly. 'I'm glad you liked it.'

'It was a very pleasant evening,' he said. 'I don't want to keep you up, though. You must be tired.'

'Not at all,' she said. 'I slept until rather late this morning, as a matter of fact.'

Philip hesitated, glancing at her. 'I suppose I couldn't ask you to play something else, then?'

She moved to the piano stool and sat down, smiling. 'Gladly. What would you like?'

He leaned on the piano and said softly, 'Anything.'

She let her hands choose the music. It was something she did when she was in an idle mood, letting the music come from her fingers without thinking about it. This time it just happened to be a rather lyrical waltz tune and Philip's face broke into a smile as he watched her.

'Strauss,' he approved, and she smiled back, nodding.

There was a movement in the doorway. Helen and Philip both glanced round casually, then the waltz stopped dead. Philip straightened from the piano, colour rushing up his face.

Drew was a hard-faced stranger, his eyes moving from one to the other in a merciless coldness.

He strolled forward into the room, yet under the light, supple movements of his body there was controlled tension which threatened to erupt at any moment.

'Oh, hallo, Drew,' said Philip with a ghastly attempt at cheerful surprise. 'I thought you were staying in Paris.'

'So did I,' Drew said very softly, silkily, and his eyes fixed on Helen.

Philip glanced at her and said awkwardly, 'Helen and I bumped into each other on the plane and I brought that kit along for Stephen and . . .'

'Goodnight, Philip,' Drew cut in coolly.

Philip opened his mouth to continue with his laboured explanation of his presence and Drew removed his cold eyes from Helen and transferred them to him. Philip almost flinched and began walking to the door like a zombie.

Helen didn't move, her hands still on the keys, her heart beating heavily, painfully.

'Well,' Philip said at the door, 'Goodnight, Helen. Thanks for the meal and the . . .' He broke off as Drew's glance touched him again and vanished as though he were a rabbit disappearing into a hat.

Silence filled the room. The closing of the front door

almost made Helen jump. She kept her eyes on the keys, her head slightly bent.

'All right,' Drew said in that soft voice, 'why?'

She lifted her head slowly and glanced in his direction without quite meeting his eyes. 'Why what?'

'Why the quick flight? You know what I mean.'

'I'd finished my shopping and there was nothing to keep me in Paris,' she said politely.

She felt the stiffening of his attitude, heard a low intake of breath. After a moment of silence he pushed his hands into his pockets. 'I see,' he said with clipped hostility.

Helen looked back at the keys and her fingers flexed.

'If you don't want that bloody lid slammed down on your hands you won't start playing again,' said Drew in a voice that made her heart stop.

She gasped at the violence and stared at him incredulously. He observed her shocked expression, smiling, lips tight. 'No,' he said. 'You won't use your damned music as a shield against me tonight.'

She put her trembling hands into her lap, her head bending again, unable to sustain her glance at him. In all the years she had known him she had never seen him like this—the amused laziness had vanished from his face and his eyes were deadly.

'You flew over with Philip? He's been here ever since?'

'He had dinner,' she said uncertainly.

'His flight was at three.' Drew glanced at his wristwatch, the movement shooting back his cuffs, exposing the strong wrist with its roughening of dark hair. 'Gone eleven—eight hours.'

'I can count,' she said defiantly. 'I haven't done

anything to be ashamed of! He came to see Stephen
and I could hardly let him leave without offering him
dinner.'

'What else did you offer him?'

She felt hot colour running up her face. Her blue
eyes flared with anger. 'Nothing!'

Drew laughed unpleasantly. 'Of course not. That's
all you've got to offer anybody, isn't it?'

He moved and she froze, her body tight and cold. He
put his hands on the top of the piano, bending towards
her. Speaking through clenched teeth he said thinly,
'You frigid little bitch.'

He was furious because she had run out on him after
last night—he had thought he had left her as he left his
other women; shattered, weak, knocked flat by his ex-
pertise.

Calling on all her reserves of strength, she turned her
head to look at him, her blue eyes freezingly cold under
the cool arch of her brows. 'Do I have to be frigid just
because you don't turn me on?'

The rage in his face was only slightly less than it had
been when she was being manhandled by the young
man in the disco. His lips curled back from his white
teeth, his eyes blazed. For a moment Helen thought he
was going to hit her. The look in his face made shivers
of sick fear run down her back. Her chin lifted defiantly, her hands clenched. She stared him out and
heard him give a long, thick inhalation. His body
seemed to lean towards her, vibrating with a desire to
hurt. Then he pulled himself back. She could almost
see the effort he made to force himself back under
control. The bones in the hard face locked rigid. His
mouth clamped together. He breathed harshly through

white nostrils. Then he swung away and stood with his back to her.

She heard her own breathing, held in the same tension, like someone waiting for a terrible pain to begin again.

Drew turned back with a mocking little smile. 'You're a liar, Helen,' he drawled. 'I turned you on all right. You were very responsive in the end.'

She burned with humiliation, unable to deny that. Searching her mind for some weapon against the knowledge in his eyes, she said with a bright pretence at the same mockery, 'Yes, I decided to find out if you were the great lover you claim you are.' Her blue eyes flicked him lightly. 'You gave me very little choice about it, but I thought I might as well find out just how good you were.'

He did not like that. Eyes narrowed, he asked acidly, 'And how do I rate?'

'I've very little experience to go on,' she said in a silvery voice. 'But it did seem slightly overrated.'

His eyes flashed but he smiled. 'You must tell me where I went wrong. Women can have such different tastes.'

Sickness tasted like acid in her throat. She wanted to fly at him, hit him, slap the smile from those hard lips. 'You're the expert,' she said, though. 'So they say.'

Her tone deliberately implied reservations about that and Drew took the note in her voice, his jaw muscles tightening. 'Maybe you need more experience,' he came back softly, with a threat in his voice.

'No, thank you,' Helen said sweetly. 'Not with you.'

She saw the anger rising inside him as though it were something visible, although Drew was keeping it very much contained, his grey eyes half shielded by his lids, his facial muscles under permanent control.

'Got someone else in mind?' he asked in a careful voice.

She did not answer, shrugging.

He thrust his hands in his pockets as if afraid of what he might do with them if they were free. 'Stay away from Philip,' he shot out thickly, 'or next time I'll hurt you—in a way you won't ever forget.'

'As long as it isn't like last night,' she said, oddly almost enjoying the pain she was feeling, as though the steely probe of the knife in her flesh was an act of love. 'I couldn't take that twice.'

Drew's face was absolutely expressionless. He stared at her in a stony silence for a long time.

'So,' he said in the familiar drawl, 'we're back to square one, are we?'

She felt the tension begin to drain out of her toes, but as it went the pain began and she twisted her hands in her lap to try to contain the agony.

Drew walked away. 'Goodnight,' he said as he went out of the door, and when she heard his footsteps crossing the hall towards the stairs Helen put her head down into her hands and shook.

Was this love? This thing inside her clawing and biting like an imprisoned animal? The wonderful emotion the poets all wrote about—was this it? Pain like fire running down her nerves, rending her like a swallowed poison?

She got up, walking carefully, like someone whose every movement meant anguish. They could keep love, she thought, as she switched out the lights. It wasn't worth the price.

She knew she wouldn't sleep. She couldn't even keep her mind on the novel she was reading. Her thoughts kept straying; with a jerk she would drag them back from the forbidden territory they had invaded, but back they would go as soon as she had removed her restraining hand. In the end she put the book down and lay in the darkness and let herself think without trying to stop it.

Pride and love warred endlessly, but Helen's pride had deep roots. It always won the battle in the end.

She slept just before dawn and woke with a little start later in a bright sunlight to hear laughter and trace it to Stephen. The door opened with a bang, followed by whispers and muffled giggles from her son. Through her lowered lashes she saw Drew and Stephen tiptoeing across the carpet. Stephen had an excited, mischievous face and Drew had a cup and saucer in his hand.

Helen pretended to be asleep. The two of them stood beside her bed for a moment, then Drew lifted Stephen up to the bed and Stephen kissed her, saying, 'Mummy, wake up, Mummy!'

She opened her eyes and smiled at him. His little arms strangled her, she heard the excitement in his voice. 'Daddy and me brought you your tea. We've been for a walk with Max. We went miles and miles right to the park and back and Max is all tired and his tongue is hanging out.'

'Poor Max,' she said, sitting up. 'Have you had your breakfast, darling?'

'Daddy and me had it together,' Stephen told her proudly. 'And we had scrambled eggs. Daddy scrambled them. He showed me how to do it, but you have to be quick and keep stirring.'

Helen's eyes flew helplessly to Drew's face, dismay in her own. 'Mrs Creel ...'

'Was delighted with her scrambled eggs,' Drew told her coolly.

'Oh,' said Helen, because Mrs Creel had a strong bias against what she called 'people in *my* kitchen'.

Stephen lay snuggled against her shoulder, his head on the smooth white skin exposed by her low-neck nightdress. He patted her bare arm. 'You're all nice and warm, Mummy.'

She felt Drew's eyes moving over her and knew she was growing more flushed, bitterly conscious of his examination of her body in the transparent silken gown.

'Aren't you getting up soon?' Stephen asked.

'Yes, when you've gone,' Helen murmured huskily.

'Our cue, I presume,' Drew said sardonically. He bent and hoisted the boy on to his shoulder and walked out, Stephen holding on to his thick, black hair for support. 'Duck,' said Drew as they went out, and Stephen ducked with his arms round Drew's neck as he avoided the door.

When they had gone, Helen felt tears spurting into her eyes. She felt lonelier than ever before in her life. The closeness between father and son emphasised her own isolation. How absurd, she scolded herself. Was she jealous?

It had never happened before. Drew had never brought Stephen in to see her in the morning. If they had been a real family they might have sat here on her bed and Drew would have kissed her too, they would have teased each other, exchanging secret little jokes over their son's head. She had seen that intimacy between parents, that silent secretive look, love given and offered back in a smile.

When she went down to breakfast, she found Drew at the table alone reading his paper. There was no sign of Stephen.

He glanced up, the grey eyes expressionless. 'Good morning.'

It was as if the little scene earlier had never taken place. She sat down and touched the coffee pot. It was hot. Pouring herself some coffee, she glanced at Drew through her lashes. How long was he intending to stay? She did not dare to ask.

'Has Stephen gone off to play-school?' she asked.

'Yes.' Drew sounded curt, abstracted.

Helen sipped her coffee.

'Don't you ever eat breakfast?' Drew demanded without looking at her, buried behind his paper.

'Not often,' she said, averting her eyes from the rack of toast, the hotplate on which the food waited.

He suddenly folded his paper and laid it on the table. Looking at her directly, he said in a clipped cold voice, 'We're going to have some new rules around here. From now on, I shall visit Stephen whenever I care to and I shall not be bringing guests with me to make things easier for you. If you don't think you can stand my presence in the house you'll have to clear off yourself.'

Helen stared at the table, trying to control the trembling of her lips.

'And when I can't get to London myself, you'll bring Stephen out to me wherever I may happen to be. I'm not letting your attitude keep me from my son any longer.'

'I've never . . .' she tried to whisper, and he cut across the unsteady words.

'We won't argue about it. Just get it through your head. I'm his father and Stephen has made it plain that he wants to see me, so he's going to see me. If that means you have to see me too, that's too bad.'

He got up and walked to the door. He had been walking away from her ever since they were married, but it had never hurt so much before. She wanted to call him back, to offer anything, however humiliating; to throw away her pride and her fear of the pain he could inflict, if only he would stay with her for a little while. But she didn't. She sat there and held her coffee cup and heard the door close with a sense of finality.

After a few moments she got up and left the room, too. She rang Janet to get a progress report on the agency and Janet sounded surprised to hear from her again so soon.

'I came back early,' Helen explained.

'How could you leave Paris if you didn't have to?' Janet wailed. 'Why is it always the people who don't want things who get them?'

Helen sounded bitter as she said, 'Or the people who do want things, who don't get them?'

There was a little pause then Janet asked tentatively, 'Something wrong, Helen?'

Pulling herself together, Helen forced a laugh. 'Of course not, just philosophising.'

'Sounds horrid,' Janet said lightly. 'I shouldn't do it again.'

Helen laughed. 'No, not on a sunny day like this one. Do you want me to take over from you to give you a break?'

'Could you?' Janet sounded delighted. 'I could take my offspring to the Zoo. I've been promising for ages.'

'Today?'

'Oh, Helen, you're an angel!'

'Then I'll use my wings and fly over to the agency now.' Helen rang off, smiling, and turned to find Drew on the bottom stair, his eyes on her.

They looked at each other blankly. 'I'm working at the agency today,' said Helen.

'So I gathered.'

She hesitated. 'Will you be here when I get back?'

His face blazed. 'Yes, I damned well will,' he said. 'Too bad.' He walked past her without looking at her and she ran her hands over her white face as the door slammed. God, was it going to be like this for ever from now on? Even in the first year of their marriage this terrible ice hadn't lain between them. Drew had teased, mocked, made fun of her, but he had never looked at her as though he hated her.

On her way to the agency she found herself obsessed with the memory of Drew's cold, intimidating face, the narrowed grey eyes which carried such dislike now when they looked at her. She had seen those eyes in so many different moods now. They had laughed, teased, smiled, grown fierce with desire, sharpened to steel— but she found she could not bear to look into them when that icy coldness lay in their depths. The casual, charming man she had known for six years had gone and left a stone-faced stranger in his place.

The agency had a pleasant, comfortable set of offices in a quiet back street off London's Oxford Street. Helen had found it exciting in the beginning to learn how to operate the switchboard, to file letters and interview both clients and prospective employees. It was always interesting to learn new skills, to discover a new world, but this morning she had to force herself to concentrate on the work. Her mind kept returning to the problem of Drew.

Should she have stayed in Paris and accepted whatever he had wanted her to accept? Could anything be worse than the situation which now existed between them?

Oh, yes, she thought miserably. It would be far worse in a little while if I let him treat me the way he treats all his other women. He would tire of his conquest and fly away to fresh fields, leaving me to eat my heart out for him.

He's angry now because he isn't used to failure. If she could believe his anger had any roots in emotion it would be different, but Drew had never even pretended to feel anything but desire for her. She couldn't let him use her like some disposable object which he wanted for the moment but would toss away when he was bored.

She was about to lock up the office when the door opened and Philip hesitantly came into the room. Helen looked at him in surprise.

'Oh, hallo, Philip.'

He stood awkwardly, his feet shifting. 'I rang the house and your housekeeper said you were here, so I thought I'd just drop in to say goodbye.'

'Goodbye?' she asked politely.

'I'm off to Durham to see my family,' he reminded her. 'Drew has given me a month's leave.'

'How nice,' she said inadequately, not knowing what

to say to him after the way the evening had broken up when Drew arrived.

He glanced at the keys in her hands. 'Were you just going?'

'Yes,' she said brightly. 'I'm in charge today, so I lock up.' She rattled the keys. 'The sign of authority.'

He smiled, then said uncertainly, 'Would you let me buy you a drink or something? Before you go home?'

'Why not?' she said. 'Just hang on while I check everything and then I'll lock up.'

Over the drink Philip said: 'Last night ...'

'Don't worry about it,' she broke in hurriedly, 'Drew was tired after his flight.'

'He looked furious.' Philip glanced at her and away, his mouth straight. 'And I can't blame him. I had no right to be there.'

'Nonsense,' she said firmly. 'You're a friend of his and he would expect me to have you to dinner while you're in London. As I say, he was tired and a little out of temper, but he was back to normal this morning.'

The lie was not easy, but she had to make Philip's troubled face clear.

'So long as I didn't cause any trouble between you,' he said. 'I'd hate to do that.'

'You didn't cause anything,' she insisted.

'I'd hate Drew to leap to conclusions,' Philip went on heavily. 'I've been there myself and I know how it can hurt.'

She swallowed, looking away. 'Yes,' she said gently. 'Don't worry, please, Philip. You haven't done any damage.'

They were parting on the pavement when Leona went past in a taxi and stared at them with narrowed, curious eyes. The taxi swerved in to the kerb, the door opened and Leona beckoned. Helen hurriedly said goodbye to Philip and moved towards the waiting vehicle.

Leona held the door open and Helen got into the taxi. As it drew away Leona glanced back through the window to see Philip on the pavement staring after them.

'Well,' she said in a faintly malicious voice, 'you're a slyboots! So there is something going on—I did wonder.'

'What are you talking about?' Helen's pale brows arched with cold hauteur and she looked at her mother with distaste.

'Come off it,' said Leona. 'And with Drew for a husband, too. But then he's not the faithful type, is he? What's sauce for the gander is sauce for the goose. I can't say I blame you. And he is a rather dishy man. How long has it been going on?'

'Nothing is going on, and I do wish you wouldn't talk like that,' Helen said wearily.

'Darling,' Leona purred, 'I'm not silly.'

Helen eyed her and half said what was in her mind, then decided better of it.

'You can tell me,' Leona said eagerly, her eyes avid. 'I wouldn't breathe a word. And, anyway, Drew could hardly complain, the life he's led for the past six years, hardly ever at home, always off around the world. And we know what he gets up to out there in Africa, don't we? I must say, Drew has never pretended to be anything but what he is.'

Helen gazed out of the window at the strolling crowds. The traffic was as heavy as usual in London in the home-going rush. She caught sight of a display of winter boots being assembled in a window and thought: heavens, is it going to be winter before the summer is even over?

The thought sent a chill down her spine. She looked up at the blue sky with yearning eyes and hated the trap she found herself in, but could not think of any way of escape.

'I rather fancied Philip myself,' Leona was saying. 'He's a widower, he told me. Was his wife pretty?'

'I never met her,' Helen said flatly.

'I was beginning to wonder if you'd ever come to life,' Leona went on, patting the lavender-rinsed hair, tucking back one curl with a listless finger. 'Such a lot of life you've wasted, Helen, with that ravishing figure of yours and your lovely hair. You could have had any number of men. Why, when you first left school I thought we were going to have some fun, because you were a gift, a positive gift, and you could have had your pick of anyone you met. But you were such a little rabbit. And after you married Drew you didn't seem to alter. But then Drew was quite a catch. Tired of him, are you?'

Helen caught the curious, interested gleam of the taxi driver's eye in his mirror and felt herself flush.

'Oh, do be quiet, Leona,' she said tightly.

Leona looked at her as though she had said something obscene. 'Why, you . . .'

Whatever she had been about to say died on her lips as Helen turned a white, angry face to her. They had halted at a road junction. 'Goodbye, Leona,' said

Helen, and without another glance dived out of the taxi and shot away into the crowd.

She had no idea what she was going to do. She had only had to get away from her mother's voice, her avid questions and slyly excited remarks. At times Helen had felt sorry for her mother in her endless quest for youth. Leona's view of life was limited by the horizon of pleasure. She was shallow, selfish, absorbed in enjoyment of the moment.

But tonight Helen felt nothing but sick distaste. Her mother had been so excited by the belief that Helen was having an affair with Philip. She seemed to want to believe it, to need to think that Helen was betraying Drew.

Such a lot of life you've wasted, Leona had said, but what she had meant had been so appalling that Helen shuddered to think of it. Leona meant that if she had had Helen's looks she would have had affairs with every man who looked at her. Helen had always known that her mother was inclined to promiscuity, but she had preferred not to notice unless it was forced upon her. She had found it degrading to imagine her mother in such situations and she had somehow made herself believe that Leona must find it humiliating too, at times, but now she saw how wrong she had been.

Leona's life revolved around the excitements of the sexual encounters she had—whether it was a brief flirtation with a stranger or a real relationship with a temporary lover. That was what Leona lived for—to her that was life. She had seen her daughter endowed with looks which Leona had envied more and more as she aged and Helen grew up. Leona had seen those looks as weapons in her war with the opposite sex and groaned to imagine Helen leaving them unused.

Had her mother ever cared for anyone? Had she ever loved Grey? Or any other of the men she had known?

Poor Grey, Helen thought. Does he know? Cheated of a real marriage, cheated of a son, the heir he needed so badly—what an empty personal life he's had. Janet had said to her long ago that she was sorry for Grey. 'He works so hard and he feels it's all for nothing.' She had been angry then, hurt, but now she felt for her father as she had never felt before. They had moved closer invisibly since Stephen's birth. Helen had given Grey the one thing he needed and she could no longer blame him for his indifference to herself, because she saw so clearly how cheated he had been in his marriage to Leona. Grey had been a bad father to her, but at least he had only been indifferent, not positively malicious. Leona's remarks had been tinged with that malice which Helen realised she had heard from her for most of her conscious life.

She had always been aware of that at some level of her mind. Malice and hostility peer through the net of words which people hand to each other. Helen had not been blind to Leona's feelings towards her, but she only realised now how much she had resented them.

She had wandered down towards the river without realising it and suddenly heard the deep voice of Big Ben intoning the hour. Listening, she gave a gasp of disbelief as she realised how late it was—she should have been home ages ago. Nine o'clock: Drew would wonder where on earth she was and he would be even angrier than he had been this morning.

She began to walk fast, her eye anxiously searching the traffic for a taxi. At last one came along free and she hailed it and gave her own address.

It was half past nine as she arrived at her home. When she got out of the taxi the door opened and she walked towards Drew with a sinking heart, her hands and feet ice-cold. He watched her with a face which terrified her, the planes of it chiselled into sharp angles, the mouth a tight cold line, the eyes leaping with rage.

CHAPTER EIGHT

His hand fastened round her arm and pulled her into the house. She looked up to stammer something conciliatory, and her voice died as she met his eyes. They were ice floes, dangerous and narrowed.

He pushed her across the hall into the drawing-room and slammed the door with his foot. His face flinty, he bit out: 'Very well, where the hell have you been?'

To her horror, Helen couldn't think of a thing to say. He petrified her. She just stared at him, her blue eyes great blank wells, her face filled with nervous helplessness.

After a terrible silence Drew asked curtly: 'You've been with Philip, haven't you?'

'Philip?' she faltered.

'Don't lie!' he shouted. 'I know you have.'

She gave him a surprised look and his mouth writhed in a sort of distaste. 'I rang your parents—I thought you must be with them. Leona took great pleasure in informing me that she'd seen you in London with Philip. Don't ever again put me in the position of having to listen to my mother-in-law gleefully hinting that you've got a lover.' Drew's voice sounded like gunfire, he spoke with the curt rattle he used when he spoke French, every word separate, clear but bitten out.

Thrusting aside the sickness of knowing that her mother had quite deliberately done this, Helen said slowly, 'Philip came to the agency as I was locking up.

He'd rung the house and Mrs Creel told him where I was, and he wanted to say goodbye before he went off to Durham.'

Drew pushed his hands into his pockets. 'So?' His mouth was a hard, straight line in his angry face. 'Did it take until now?'

'We had a drink for about twenty minutes and as I was saying goodbye to him, Leona went past in a taxi and stopped, and I left Philip and joined her.' Helen stopped speaking, her face filling with the sick distaste she had felt ever since she spoke to Leona. 'We ... we quarrelled and I got out and then I just walked around. I forgot the time. I'm sorry.'

Her silence was unbroken for a moment. Drew stared with narrowed, probing eyes. 'What did you quarrel with Leona about? I thought she sounded oddly vicious when I talked to her.'

Helen shrugged wearily. 'She made some unpleasant remarks and I objected to them.'

'What sort of remarks?'

'Oh, don't ask,' she said, turning away.

'About Philip?'

She nodded.

'I see,' Drew commented flatly. 'You don't need to cross any t's or dot any i's. I get the picture. Your mother is a bitch.'

Helen shivered, wrapping her arms around her body.

'What did Philip have to say?'

She started. Drew had spoken quietly, having moved nearer, and she had not realised that he was so close. Now she looked at him with anxious eyes.

'He was disturbed because he realised you were annoyed last night when you found him here. He wanted to make sure he ...' She broke off, biting her lip.

'He what?' Drew asked pointedly.

'He hadn't caused any trouble,' she finished hurriedly. 'He didn't want to think he might have hurt you the way he was hurt.'

'And you told him he hadn't,' Drew said drily.

'Yes.' Their eyes met and she looked away.

'Yes,' Drew agreed softly. 'And of course, it's the truth. Philip is an irrelevance. He's the salt in the wound.'

She gave him a puzzled, searching look, but he turned away. 'You must be starving if you haven't eaten. I told Mrs Creel to hold dinner until you got home. Shall we eat?'

Mrs Creel was in a frosty mood, furious at the disruption of her routine. Helen apologised to her with a faintly pleading smile. She liked to maintain good relations with her staff, and she valued Mrs Creel's abilities highly. She was relieved when a reluctant smile was given back to her.

'You work too hard, Mrs Lincoln,' the housekeeper said with a scolding note in her voice. 'You look washed out to me.'

'I'm a little tired, that's all,' Helen said, aware that Drew was watching her with narrowed eyes, and instinctively defending her inner misery from his probing stare.

When Mrs Creel had gone he said quietly, 'She's right. You look half dead.'

'I don't like quarrelling with people,' she said, bending her neck with a faint, defensive movement.

'Play for me, after dinner,' Drew said with an odd

irony. 'That will lift you out of your mood. Music always gets to you.' He gave her a strange little smile. 'Even if nothing else does.'

After dinner, she sat at the piano as she had last night with Philip, her hands flexed on the keys, her mind empty, waiting for whatever her fingers should choose to play, not making any deliberate choice herself.

It surprised her to find Rachmaninov coming passionately into the room. She rarely played his music, but tonight she heard it leaping like fire under her fingers.

Behind her, Drew sat upright on the couch, staring at her. She heard him take a deep breath and hoped he did not make any connections. Then she lost consciousness of him, aware of nothing but the music, hearing it in her blood, the unconscious technique of her long fingers falling from her mind as the music took it over. Technique was a necessary function of the brain which had to become second nature if one was ever to play as the music was intended to be played. Her hands did their job without thinking and the music flowed through her body to fill the silent room, filled with a passion she had never known before. When she ended, she was trembling.

Slowly she turned to face Drew and found him regarding her blankly. After a moment he said: 'You really should have taken it up professionally. I've heard a good many lesser performances in concert halls.' Rising, he walked to the door and she stared at his departing back with a sense of regret which she had felt for what seemed like eternity. 'Goodnight,' he said flatly.

Next day he told her without any particular intonation that he had been thinking of changing his whole

work pattern. 'I'm giving up constant site visits. Someone else can take over the field work. I shall stay in
London and stick to admin.'

Helen knew she was almost trembling, her eyes fixed
on his face in anxious scrutiny. Why was he doing it?
What was his motive? He met her stare levelly without
giving anything away.

'It will solve the problem of what to do about
Stephen,' he said. 'He'll be starting full-time school
soon, won't he? We wouldn't want to disrupt his education.'

Helen could not think of anything to say in reply.
Drew waited for a moment, watching her, then his
mouth straightened into a set smile.

'Sorry if it inconveniences you, of course,' he told
her with a coldness that stung. 'You'll have to put up
with my constant presence in the house, I'm afraid.'

He walked away without waiting for her to respond
this time, and she wished she knew what was going on
inside his head, but Drew was too good at hiding things.
Whatever his real motive for this change, she knew she
would never guess.

His presence, although now permanent, was not
really constant. He worked as hard in his London office
as he had on site, leaving early in the morning and
coming home tired just in time to change and have a
drink before dinner. Some evenings he did not come
home at all. She realised he must be seeing other
women—it was the obvious explanation and she had
expected it, but she hated knowing what was going on,
and she found herself looking at him next day with
jealous, miserable eyes and fighting to keep her feelings
out of her face.

His manner to her had returned, more or less, to the cool charm of their first meetings. When they were alone at dinner Drew talked to her about his work, about Stephen, about her music, and Helen responded warily without warmth. She still kept him at a distance, but there was no need. The caressing intimacy never entered Drew's eyes for her. He had stopped teasing her. Whatever had made his eyes gleam with that masculine amusement when he looked at her had gone.

Leona, of course, put a very different construction on his permanent presence in London. 'Drew soon put a stop to what was going on between you and Philip, didn't he?' she asked maliciously. 'He leaves nothing to chance. If I were you ...'

'But you're not me,' Helen snapped, walking away.

She could not stand listening to her mother's innuendoes. Fortunately Leona rarely bothered to see her. It was usually Grey who came to the house. He came to see Stephen almost daily. The relationship between Helen and her father had deepened so gradually, so infinitesimally, that she had hardly noticed the point at which they passed beyond polite indifference into a guarded warmth.

She recognised now that Grey was as wary of commitment as she was herself—both of them frightened of rejection, wary of pain. He had slowly put out feelers towards her since Stephen's birth, groping tentatively towards a genuine relationship, and she suspected that Grey had been relieved, by Stephen's arrival, of the fanatical resentment he had felt because he had no son. Stephen had altered his world, given meaning to his life, just as had happened to her. For both of them it was easier to show love towards Stephen than to anyone else. Children made it so easy to give love—they greeted it as a plant greets the sun; eagerly, openly, without reservation. There were none of the complicating sensitivities which can bedevil the expression of love between adults.

Once Grey said uncomfortably, 'Everything all right between you and Drew now, eh?'

She had lied. What else could she do? 'Yes,' she had smiled, and seen the relief in her father's face.

'I did worry about him at the start,' he confessed. 'Always was a lad with women, but I suppose it was wild oats. He's over that now.'

Was he? she had thought drily. He was still spending a number of evenings out of the house and she had no idea where he went, nor any intention of asking. In fact, she was sometimes relieved that he stayed out. She found his presence a strain. She felt she was on a see-saw, moving between a jealous desire to have him under her eyes and a weary feeling that it was easier not to see him at all.

Some evenings he insisted that Helen should accompany him when he went out—they dined, went to a theatre or to a party, in much the same way that they always had when he was in London.

In the company of his friends, Helen smiled and tried to look as though she were enjoying herself, but when she met Drew's cool, ironic stare she knew she was not fooling him.

While he was away in Africa for months, she had been able to forget him; put him at the back of her mind, out of sight and out of memory. Now he had refused to be put away into that locked compartment. He had forced himself into the foreground of her life and she found it impossible to forget him. The black head moved through the rooms of their home. The grey eyes watched her unreadably. Looking at him across tables, at parties, hearing his feet on the stairs, she found him dominating her mind.

He spent a good deal of time at weekends with Stephen. Helen had the choice of either making a third in their party or staying out of it—and the choice was in practice always decided for her. Stephen made his point with the insistent tenacity of a child. 'Mummy come too,' he said bluntly with a note in his voice which made it impossible for her to make excuses for refusing. She had to pretend to want to come for Stephen's sake and Drew knew it.

She suspected he was amusing himself by forcing her to accept his company. 'We'll go to the sea today,' he would say without even looking at her, and she would have to smile as Stephen jumped up and down and clapped his hands in delight.

She hated those visits to the sea. Grey had a small bungalow by the sea at a village near Rye. They always took salad, cold meat and fruit in a hamper with them and ate a picnic lunch on the great sandy dunes with the wind whistling through the marram grass and the cold rush of the sea a few feet away. Stephen either ran nervously in and out of the shallow waves or built sandcastles with his eyes fixed on the water. Drew in dark trunks would lie on the beach and stare at Helen until the hair on the back of her neck prickled with awareness and resentment. His cool stare wandered over her body in her brief swimsuit, never touching her face. Their eyes rarely met, yet she was as conscious of those slow, intentional examinations as if he were a surgeon with a knife.

Once or twice she refused to change in the bungalow to swim and Stephen infuriatingly demanded: 'Why, Mummy? Why?'

Drew's mouth curled in derisive mockery. 'Yes,' he murmured. 'Why, Helen?'

She did not answer him, but after that she always changed when they did and bore the crucifixion of his gaze with as much nerve as she could muster.

'Play ball,' Stephen would demand, easily bored even with the exciting business of building sandcastles, and then Helen would be forced to get up and play with them with those narrowed eyes on her body as she ran to get the ball or leapt up to catch it.

Even more than that, she hated to watch Drew eyeing one of the other women on the beach, his experienced speculative eyes roving over their salt-bloomed bodies as they walked past. Jealousy had become so much a part of her daily world that the returning stab of it was like the tide turning in its eternal cycle. She did not need to see him with other women to know how he looked at them, to imagine the mocking tone of that voice as he teased them.

'You're getting quite a tan,' Drew said one late afternoon, glancing along the smooth gleam of her thighs in a way which made her tense. He was sitting beside her, his knees up, his hands locked round them, his black head leant against them, the grey eyes on her. The wind from the sea lifted the black hair and blew it softly back in a ruffled plume. She glanced quickly at him and found her throat dry at the impression she took in of the long, sand-dusted legs, the brown chest and broad bronzed shoulders.

'I don't tan easily.'

'No,' he agreed. 'Your skin is too fair.' His hand moved, the long fingers touched her thigh, slid silkily inward, and she jerked away as though the touch burnt her.

Drew laughed without humour. He sprang to his feet and called Stephen. 'Time to go,' he said, and the child wailed in protest.

He was fast asleep, though, by the time they reached London. He had to be carried into the house, fast asleep in a tartan travelling rug, his face pink and relaxed with the salt and sun flush on his cheeks. Drew carried him easily, looking down at him with an indulgent smile. Helen's heart stopped as she watched him.

My God! she thought sickeningly. I'm even jealous because he smiles at Stephen like that. When the hard, cool face wore that smile she felt her senses quickening with a fever she could not ease. Drew's smile was heart-wrenching. She ached to have it turned to her, to find that look back in his eyes. She followed him as he went into the house and knew she was almost on the point of going to him in humiliating weakness and offering whatever he wanted.

That evening he took her to a party given by some friends of his who lived on the north of London in a semi-rural suburb heavily ringed with trees to give the impression of being still the little country area it had been long ago before London spilled out in that direction.

The drive took longer than Drew had planned since for some reason traffic flowing north had been heavier than usual. As they rose out of London through Highgate, the lights of the city below seemed to fill the sky with an orange glow like the reflection of fire, or the dying embers of a smoky sunset.

The party had spilled out from the detached mock-Georgian house into the garden where a barbecue was going on under the trees. A large man in a white chef's hat was superintending the production of rather burnt steaks and chops. He waved an enormous fork at them as they passed, shouting, 'Hey, Drew! Care to take over?'

'No, thanks,' said Drew, laughing. 'I'll leave that to you.'

Roy Dryden was one of his London executives, a heavily built man with a slight tonsure at the back of his brown head. He leaned towards casual clothes, to-night wearing a T-shirt on which a virulent green spider sprawled.

His wife, Carol, was a vivacious woman of around thirty, her auburn hair curling around a heavily made-up face, her eyes accentuated by glittering green make-up. She greeted Drew by throwing her arms around him and kissing his mouth lingeringly. 'Now I know it's a party,' she said, smiling into his eyes. 'We couldn't have one without you.'

Her greeting to Helen was less exuberant and politely curious. She admired Helen's red-and-black chiffon evening blouse, her black velvet skirt. 'You always look ravishing,' she told her, yet with that little note of doubt which Drew's friends always seemed to have in their voices when they spoke to her. They could not quite make up their minds about her. She was so reserved, so withdrawn, that they felt uneasy in

her company and try as she might she could not make
herself behave with the casual noisy good humour they
all displayed.

Helen did not like parties. She was shy and found it
hard to make conversation with a stranger. The noise,
the crowds of people, alarmed her. She had never told
Drew. He seemed to enjoy them, easily entering into
the banter and lighthearted chat. Helen suffered from
a form of claustrophobia at parties, feeling herself hemmed in by strangers, her mind threatened. She was an
introvert; reserved, nervous, afraid to come out from
behind her sheltering defences and expose herself to
ridicule or failure. She had learnt to hide it behind a
cool manner, using pride as a shield, without ever being
able to deal with the other problems that caused.
People imagined that her set, stiff face implied superi-
ority when in fact it implied the opposite. She was
aware that her manner produced this effect—but did
not know how to dispel the impression.

That evening she was separated from Drew early on
and found herself hovering on the edge of little groups,
trying to think of something to say without any success.
Some of the men, particularly those who did not know
she was Drew's wife, tried to talk to her and gave up
under the glazed blankness of her blue eyes.

She wandered out into the garden and inhaled the
aromatic smoke from the barbecue. There was a little
crowd of people still round it, talking as they sampled
Roy's food, and a host of midges danced around them,
glittering like fireflies in the lamplight. The trees had
been decked with coloured fairy lights, giving the
garden a magical carnival air. A great pale-winged

moth fluttered uneasily backwards and forwards as though drawn irresistibly by the light.

Helen stood under one tree and felt totally shut out from the party atmosphere. Her eye wandered around the faces of the people at the barbecue and then moved on towards the house. Suddenly she caught sight of Drew leaning under another of the trees, his black head bent over a girl in a blue shirt and trousers. Helen had seen Drew dancing with her in the house. Now they were talking intimately, looking at each other in a way which made her feel sick.

Drew turned his head as though suddenly becoming aware of being watched and across the shadowy garden his eyes met Helen's. His face betrayed nothing but cool scrutiny of her own.

She stared back at him, conscious of that sickening stab of pain. The girl's hand was running up and down his arm. She was talking, smiling. Drew looked away from Helen and smiled at the girl. He bent his head and with an intolerable wrench she saw him kiss the dark red mouth.

Helen turned and walked back into the house very fast. Inside her now she was being eaten alive with a jealousy she could not bear. Her face was set in white lines.

She had to get out of there before she made a public fool of herself. She didn't even see the people she passed, her eyes turned inward on that scene beneath the shadow of the tree.

'Helen?'

The voice, the hand on her arm, meant nothing to her for a moment. She managed to turn her blonde head and looked at the man who had stopped her, with a smile fixed to her lips which merely emphasised the shock of her inner pain.

'What is it?'

She looked at him properly then and recognised Philip with a start. 'Philip,' she said hoarsely, 'take me home.'

There were others in the room and she never even saw them. Her eyes stayed in pleading on Philip's brown face. He looked taken aback, worried, horrified.

'What's wrong?' he asked in a low voice.

'Please,' Helen just managed to whisper, 'take me home.'

She could never even remember afterwards how Philip got her out of that house and into his car. They drove away and cold air came rushing in on her face, waking her from the traumatic shock, making her gasp.

'Is it too cold for you? Close it,' said Philip, giving her an anxious look. 'Do you feel ill? You're so white.'

'He was kissing someone,' she said because she could not lock it inside herself any longer. She had to let the pain spill out or it would eat at her for ever.

Philip took a deep breath. 'Drew?' he asked, unnecessarily.

Helen heard herself laughing and winced at the sound she was making. It did not sound like her, that high shrill noise. 'Who else?' she asked bitterly. 'It's one thing to know—another to be forced to watch, and he did it quite deliberately. He knew I was there. He did it for me to see. He wanted to make me see.'

Philip suddenly spun off the main road and pulled up in a dimly lit suburban street. He turned and gave her a troubled, uncertain look. 'I'm sure it meant nothing, Helen.'

'Of course it meant nothing,' she flung back wildly. 'Nothing ever does with Drew. She was just one of a long procession.'

Philip had incredulity in his eyes. 'Not since he married you, Helen.'

'Since he married me,' she said on a sharp, jealous note. 'I'm sick of it! He was making sure I saw so that I'd know what I was passing up.'

Staring at her, Philip said dazedly, 'But I thought your marriage was idyllic. Drew's mad about you. Everyone knows. He used to be the life and soul of a party, but since he married you, he's changed.'

'Whitewashing,' she snapped. She caught Philip's disturbed stare and put her hands over her face, shuddering. 'Oh, I'm sorry, I'm sorry, I shouldn't have burdened you with all this . . . forget it, Philip. Will you take me home, please?'

Philip didn't move, his hands on the wheel, his eyes fixed on her. 'What you need is a drink,' he said flatly.

Helen struggled with a rending desire to cry. Biting her lip, she said huskily, 'Or failing that, a long jump off a high bridge.'

'Don't!' exclaimed Philip, amazed, shocked. 'Don't ever think such a thing! My God, Helen . . .' He broke off and she shook her head in self-disgust.

'I'm sorry—that was a childish, stupid thing to say. Yes, Philip, I could do with a drink. I could do with one badly.'

He took her to a club he knew, apologising because it was not the sort of place he would have taken her to normally, but at this hour he could not think of anywhere else. They sat in a gloomily lit corner and stared into their drinks. The muffled music had a hectic beat and a girl singer in a tight, low-cut red dress sang smokily in a small spotlight.

'Have you and Drew quarrelled lately?' Philip asked, and Helen felt the tentative look he was giving her and read it.

She looked at him drily. 'Not over you, Philip, don't worry.'

He flushed. 'I just thought Drew might have some crazy idea that I'd been paying you attentions.' His brown eyes moved to his drink. 'He could be jealous.'

'No,' she said coolly, 'it isn't that.'

Philip kept his eyes on his glass. 'Sure?' He shot her a quick look and then looked back at his glass. 'I suppose it could have looked that way.'

'No,' she said.

'Drew's very quick,' Philip muttered. He paused, his hesitation palpable. 'Oh, what's the point of beating around the bush? I find you very attractive, Helen, and I don't think Drew missed it.'

She flushed slightly and made a face. 'No,' she admitted then, 'he didn't miss it.'

Philip swallowed. 'So you did know?'

The singer was getting a languid ripple of applause. The band swung into a dance tune and some couples drifted on to the floor. Helen looked at them and stood up. 'Let's dance,' she said.

Philip had an astonished look as he slowly rose. They moved on to the floor and danced politely. 'Did you have a good holiday in Durham?' she asked.

'Very.' His hand shifted on her back restlessly. 'I'm

flying back to Kowoli in two days. I hadn't expected to
see you at the party tonight—you don't usually turn up.
I did imagine I'd see Drew.'

'Yes,' she said drily, 'you would have done.'

'He likes to keep in touch,' said Philip, as though
defending Drew. 'It's sometimes easier to do that in a
social setting. It makes it so formal to talk in the office
or on the site. There's such a different atmosphere.'

That had never occurred to her. The dance ended
and they walked back to their table. They had another
drink and Philip talked about Kowoli and then about
Durham and his family.

'It was good to get home, but I'm looking forward to
getting back to work. Holidays get tedious after a
while.'

'You know that Drew has decided to stay mostly in
London now?'

Philip nodded. 'Word got around.' He stared at her.
'That has to be because of you, Helen. It has to be.'

'Or because Drew is finally tired of jetsetting around
and working on hot, dusty sites out in the middle of
nowhere.'

Philip did not reply to that. He glanced at his watch.
'I think we'd better go—it's half past one. Drew will
half kill me if he gets back before we do.'

'You really think that's likely?' she asked with bitter
irony. 'He's probably in bed with that girl by now.'

Philip winced and she hated herself for saying that.
She had no right to say such things to him. She had
shut it all in for years and now she didn't seem able to
stop it blurting out, all the jealousy and pain and
misery she had hidden away for years.

'I'm tearing apart,' she said to Philip. 'Cracking up.

It was easier when he stayed out of sight and I could pretend it wasn't anything to do with me, but I can't stand watching him walk away from me all the time, guessing where he is, imagining what he's doing.'

'That's the worst part,' Philip said heavily. 'I know —my God, I know. Julia showed me what a vivid imagination I could have. I never thought I had one before. At school they used to put on my reports: lacks imagination. Hell, they should have seen me when I realised what had been going on while I wasn't around to see.'

'Does it ever stop hurting?' she asked him.

Philip grimaced. 'I hope so. In my case, hurt isn't quite the right word. Humiliation—that's all I feel now. I was the fool who didn't know what was going on, that's what burns me up now. You can stand a lot of things, but it's hard to forgive being made to look a fool in front of your friends.'

He turned and gave her a direct glance. 'You ought to talk to Drew, Helen. I think you're wrong. You ought to give him a chance to tell you so.'

She felt calmer now, the ache lessened by having talked about it. 'You're very kind, Philip. I am grateful.'

He took her hand and kissed it lightly. 'It's very easy to be kind to you, Helen—that's the trouble. I would like to be a lot more than kind and I've a shrewd idea Drew knows that. He's not an easy man. You couldn't expect him to be—he's head and shoulders above almost everyone I've ever met. He's clever, tough and quickwitted, and he can be the kindest man on earth. When I went crazy after Julia died, I lived on Drew's strength for weeks. I owe him a hell of a lot and I've played him a rotten trick by falling for you. I hate myself.'

'I promise you, it made no difference,' Helen said earnestly. 'Drew himself said as much.' She smiled at him faintly. 'And I don't think you have fallen for me, Philip—not really. You just have this image of me. It's what you need at the moment, but it isn't real. I'm not a marble lady on a pedestal, I'm a human being with faults and problems of my own. When you get out to Kowoli, you'll soon forget I ever existed.'

Philip looked wryly at her. 'If you say so, Helen.'

It was nearly half past two when he parked outside her home. He turned and gave her a slight smile. 'Feel better?'

'Almost normal,' she said brightly. She leaned forward to kiss his cheek. 'Thank you, Philip.'

He touched her face lingeringly, staring at her. 'I've got to say this—you're the most beautiful woman I've ever seen and it's going to take me a long, long while to forget you, Helen.'

She felt tears at the back of her eyes. Apart from Drew, Philip was the only man who had ever come within light years of touching her feelings. She was not in love with him, but she liked him very much and she felt involved with him. 'I won't forget you, either,' she promised.

He leaned forward slowly and she met his mouth without holding back, her hands framing his face.

Behind her the door was flung open suddenly and she found herself being dragged from the car. She looked at Drew in startled surprise for a moment, then her face froze over.

He wasn't even looking at her. Philip had climbed

out of the car and was coming round towards him. He
never got there. Drew lunged for him with a snarl and
Helen heard the vicious connection of his fist with
Philip's jaw. Philip fell backwards across the bonnet
and Drew lifted him, his hand clutching Philip's shirt.
As he drew back his arm to drive it into Philip's face
again, Helen flew at him, pummelling him with her
fists.

'How dare you? How dare you?' she cried in rage.

Drew's head swung. He stared at her, breathing
thickly, his eyes leaping with the same murderous rage
she had seen in them before.

'You have no right,' she said confusedly.

'No right?' Drew threw the words back in a blurred
hoarseness, running them together as though he could
scarcely speak. 'You think I'm going to stand by and let
him take you?' The hard mouth moved violently.
'Think again!'

'You kissed someone else—you meant me to see it,'
she said bitterly. 'Well, I saw, and if you can, I can.'

Drew's hand released its grip on Philip's shirt and
Philip fell back, a hand at his bleeding lip.

Helen had never seen Drew totally at a loss for words
before, but she saw it now. He was staring at her fixedly
and looking as though he wanted to break things.

Philip straightened and moved and Drew turned on
him as though glad to have something he could do,
spitting words at him fiercely. 'As for you, if I catch
you within a mile of her again I'll kill you, and those
aren't just empty words. You'd better believe it.'

'I do,' said Philip with a slight grimace, touching his
swelling, bruised lip and then his jaw. 'I may not talk
again for weeks.'

'Just stay away from her,' Drew said tautly.

Philip gave Helen a strange, brief look. 'Goodbye, Helen.' He turned and got into his car and it fired with a roar and disappeared with winking tail lights.

Helen turned towards the house and Drew's hand shot out to grab her arm. 'Not so fast,' he ground out.

'I'm not shouting at you out here,' she said coldly, and walked into the house with him striding beside her like a leopard tensing for a spring.

CHAPTER NINE

THE silence between them was full of anger. She walked into the drawing-room and turned to face him, her eyes filled with the jealousy she could no longer hide, her face white. 'I'm tired,' she said with a snap. 'Can you say whatever you've got to say quickly?'

'No, I damned well can't,' Drew told her in a burning rage, his face all sharp angles, as though the bones were locked together in a fierce temper.

She laced her shaking fingers together and assumed a patient air. 'Very well, get it over with.'

'Don't take that tone with me!' Drew sounded as though it needed very little to push him over the edge into outright violence and she looked at him with a consuming desire to give him that push, to make the explosive atmosphere between them go up in a flash of white-hot rage that would satisfy some nagging need to make Drew touch her.

He drew a long breath. 'What's been going on between you and Philip?'

'We had a few drinks and danced,' she said deliberately, her eyes on his face.

She saw his mouth harden. The grey eyes leapt with flame. 'And then what? Do you know what the time is? Where have you been?' He took a breath which seemed to make his chest heave. 'What have you been doing?'

'Use your imagination,' she mocked.

Drew shot forward with a sound like the snarl he

176

had given when he hit Philip. 'You little bitch,' he muttered in that thick, hoarse voice, his hands grabbing her shoulders, shaking her as if she were a limp rag doll. 'Has he had you? Tell me! Has he?'

Helen's heart was beating fiercely against her chest. She looked at Drew's face with incredulous eyes.

'Tell me!' Drew burst out raggedly, and she silently shook her head, trembling.

He gave a smothered groan, staring at her, then his mouth was rammed down against hers so painfully that she felt blood seep into her mouth from her inner lip. Drew's hands handled her ruthlessly, bruising, gripping, as though he wanted to hurt her, but she heard the heavy thud of his heart above her own and her body slackened in surrender as she listened to it, as though the rhythm were passing into her own blood.

Her hands slid slowly round his neck and her lips parted. With a hungry sound, Drew gathered her closer, kissing her deeply, holding her body against his own with both arms locked round her.

Her lips trembled. She kissed him back, tentatively exploring his mouth as he had explored hers, feeling his arms tighten, hearing his heartbeat race away.

A nervous, reluctant hope was filling her mind. She pushed her fingers into his hair and heard him give a stifled gasp of pleasure.

At last he lifted his head, his eyes half closed. 'Why?' he asked huskily. 'Why did you do it? What do you think I felt when I realised you'd walked out of the party?'

'What did you expect me to do? Turn a blind eye to what you were doing?' As she spoke her jealousy rushed back like a flood of acid in her throat and it showed in her face, in the burning blue of the eyes fixed on him, in the trembling anger of her voice. 'You did it deliberately so that I could see.'

'Yes,' he said sharply. 'Don't tell me you gave a damn.'

'I won't,' she lied, but her face gave her away and Drew leant towards her almost pleadingly.

'Say you cared. My God, do you have to be told how I feel? Did it matter to you? I had to know. I kissed her and when I looked round you'd gone and I didn't know if you'd been indifferent or if it had meant anything to you.'

'I hated it,' she said fiercely, abandoning her pretence.

Drew closed his eyes. 'Oh, God,' he groaned. 'Helen. Why didn't you stay, why did you go like that? And with Philip! Half the party saw the two of you leaving together. Can you imagine what they thought? I had to look as if I wasn't bothered a hair while all the time I was going through hell.'

'At least you know how it feels,' she said angrily. 'I've been doing it for years.'

Drew looked at her almost blankly. 'What?'

She wanted to hit him, to tear at him with her nails, her jealousy flung into his handsome face.

It would be a terrible relief to admit it all, to let her shield drop and no longer need to fight to hide the way she felt. But she wouldn't. She looked at him with a face torn between love and anger and Drew said urgently, 'Tell me, Helen.'

She would not answer, turning her face away. He bent and said huskily, 'Shall I tell you? Do you need to be told? You know, don't you, what it did to me to see you in his arms, to watch him touching you, kissing you. You have to know it tears me apart to think of any other man near you.'

The harshness in the later words got through to her. She turned back to look searchingly into his strained face.

'I love you,' Drew muttered under his breath.

'No,' she said shakily.

His head came up and his lips were white. 'Yes,' he said as if he flung the word at her. Helen could not let herself believe it. It was too agonisingly sweet to believe. She stood there with pain tearing through her, pulsing in her blood, and stared at him hungrily.

'I don't even know when it started,' Drew muttered. 'At first I just felt irritated because you so obviously disliked me and I fancied you. I married you for a number of reasons, most of them selfish. It wasn't for a long time that I would admit to myself that one of my reasons was a need to make sure you didn't marry anybody else. I don't think I loved you then—I just wanted you.' His grey eyes flared. 'You have a lovely body and I wanted it badly.'

She remembered their wedding night and looked at him with narrowed suspicion. Drew caught the look and his mouth went wry.

'Yes,' he said heavily, 'I admit that was the basic reason why I made you sleep with me that first time. It's true, Grey wanted heirs, but even more than that, I wanted you.' His eyes held a feverish glitter. 'I know you hated it, but I'm not going to lie this time—I enjoyed it. Even though you fought me, I loved every minute of it. I'd been waiting to get you into bed for months and when I did, I went crazy.'

Helen felt her skin burn as she recalled the moan of his voice as he made love to her.

'And then next morning you really let me have it. I could almost have curled up and rolled away like a hedgehog. If you knew how small you made me feel! The night I'd found so fantastic had just been an ordeal to you! I wouldn't admit to myself how that stung. I came back next night and I'd had to drink to make myself do it, and when you cried I felt like crying myself.'

'You'd behaved abominably,' she told him.

'I knew that and I hated myself. So I cleared off and you had the baby and I hoped he would soften you, but there was no sign of any change. I kept going away and coming back and getting the same frigid reception. The ice stayed solid.'

'What did you expect? Don't tell me there weren't others during those years?'

He flushed and shrugged. 'At the start there were— I needed to forget the humiliation of being so ruthlessly turned down.'

He felt her stirring in his arms and looked at her anxiously. 'That all stopped years ago. How could I take a woman to bed when I couldn't even raise any enthusiasm for it? All I could think about was you. I was reduced to bringing home people who bored me to tears just to have an excuse to keep you in London. I rang you from Africa with blatant excuses about being concerned over Stephen's latest cold. My God, I made a bloody fool of myself and you never even noticed.'

'Are you telling me there hasn't been anyone else lately?' she asked in an attempt at irony which sounded far too much like pleading.

'There hasn't,' he said quickly. 'Not for years. Oh, I've taken someone out now and then—dinner, dancing, a theatre trip. But I just didn't want them. I used to think of sex as an appetite like any other. Well, mine had gone. I got more of a kick out of hearing your voice over the phone than I could ever have got out of a night with the most dazzling female.' He looked at her and she felt her heart turn over. 'So I had to learn patience. It wasn't easy. Then Stephen talked to me and I got the fright of my life. I thought someone else had got in first. I flew to Paris to see what was really happening and one look at you told me that the ice was still in place. What you said about Farrier told me he wasn't your lover.'

She laughed. 'Poor James, how horrified he'd be to hear you say such a thing! He's far too conventional for that.'

Drew's hard mouth lifted in a quick smile. 'That's saved his life. When I was on my way from Jamaica to Paris I was planning his violent assassination.'

She laughed again and Drew bent his head down suddenly and kissed her mouth hard.

'Darling,' he whispered. 'My darling. Say you care, just a little. I can't eat my heart out for you any longer.' He caught her and pushed his face into her hair. 'That night in Paris I thought at last I'd got you, and then you ran away and I went crazy not knowing why.'

'I thought you just wanted to sleep with me,' she said unevenly. 'I thought I'd just be one of your women, and no way was I going to be put in that position.'

'There are no other women,' he said roughly. 'Do you want me to swear it on a stack of bibles? When I realised you'd been on the same plane with Philip I was terrified. I'd seen the way he looked at you. I knew you liked him more than you've ever liked anyone else—you're usually so stiff with men. Philip seemed to get through to you—and I was sick with jealousy.'

'I like him,' she said. 'No more.'

'I hope that's true,' said Drew with a twist of the mouth. 'Because Philip has been a friend of mine for years and I never thought I'd get to the stage of wanting to cave his head in like an eggshell.'

'Poor Philip,' she said, leaning on him. 'You hit him very hard tonight.'

'He was lucky. What I wanted to do was run him over with his damned car.' Drew tightened his arms round her. 'He kissed you, and for that I could have cheerfully killed him.'

'It was your own fault! You kissed that girl!'

His lips brushed her cheek, her ear, her hair. 'Darling, were you jealous?'

'Sick with it,' she whispered shakily.

'Helen,' he said hoarsely, 'tell me you love me.'

She put her arms round his neck. 'Take me to bed and I'll tell you there,' she murmured with a husky laughter in her voice.

She heard his caught breath and then his answering laughter. 'A more wanton invitation I've never had,' he mocked, but his voice was unsteady.

As she lay in bed looking at the golden gleam of his skin she ran her lips down his body and whispered, '*Je t'aime*.'

Drew gave a groan and lifted her head to kiss her. As his lips reluctantly parted from hers, he said wickedly,

'Your French needs some practice, as I recall from Paris. I must teach you a few handy phrases—a woman needs a good vocabulary for these occasions.'

'Yours is far too extensive,' she complained.

His eyes were amused. 'One picks it up,' he agreed teasingly. 'Repeat after me: *J'ai envie de toi, mon amour.*'

Her blue eyes deepened to a rich purple as she whispered the words and Drew came down to her with a long groan.

That night for the first time, Helen discovered the true meaning of sensation; her fingers, lips, body given lessons in a sensuality which turned her to shivering fire. Drew held his own needs on a tight rein while he encouraged hers to have full sway. She learnt how her caress could move him, how it could excite her. As her passion rose, Drew calmed her, whispering, 'Softly, softly, my darling. Don't rush it. We have all the time in the world.'

There was no time, she thought dazedly, aware of a need which drove her crazy. There was no world—except this small room and their bodies creating a harmony which made all other music seem suddenly pointless.

'Drew, I love you,' she sobbed, burying her face in him, entwined with him. The sensation his skilful love-making had aroused had twisted to an intolerable pleasure. 'Now, *chérie*,' Drew gasped, and the necessity of release became extreme, the flames leaping up to consume them both.

Later, wrapped in his arms, drained and blissful, she let her hands decipher the smile on his face, her fingers reading every line delicately. 'How many years I've wasted,' she groaned. 'I think I could have loved you from the start.'

'What stopped you?' he asked drily.

'Leona,' she said, and told him what she had overheard. 'I wasn't going to give you the satisfaction of breaking my heart.'

Drew looked at her angrily. 'Look, my darling, there was no conspiracy. I wouldn't have dreamed of discussing you with your mother. Any plot was in her head, not mine.'

All the same, she thought, if she had let herself fall hard for Drew in the beginning, he might well have taken whatever he could and walked away because he had admitted he wasn't in love at the start.

Drew caressed her bare shoulder with his lips. 'When did you fall in love with me, Helen?'

'I don't know,' she admitted. 'I never remember thinking: I'm in love. It just grew on me.'

'Same here,' he agreed. 'We attracted each other from the start, I suppose, and only fell in love gradually. I knew several years ago. It happened one night when I was looking at you at the piano and I realised I was actually jealous of the damned thing because you never looked like that when you looked at me.' He laughed sharply. 'Jealous of a piano! I felt an idiot.'

'I don't know when I realised,' she said. 'I refused to admit it for a very long time. Even when I did, it was only in a tacit way to myself. I wouldn't let myself think about it, I shut it out of my mind as much as I could.'

'You shut me out pretty ruthlessly,' he said with a harsh intonation. 'I've been hovering around out there like a lovesick fool for what seems like years. Making up lies to give myself a reason for seeing you, fighting

down a need to touch you. Smiling as though it was all
great fun when what I wanted to do was get on my
knees and beg.'

She looked at him through her lashes, humour in
her eyes. 'I don't remember much begging being done
the night in Paris. You just grabbed.'

He laughed thickly. 'I was angry enough to feel I
didn't give a damn whether you wanted it or not.' He
ran his hand down her body with a groan. 'God, it was
fantastic, though. You really turned me on—I was
walking on air next morning. I rushed poor old Philip
out of the apartment to get rid of him and I was coming
back to take you out to dinner. I thought at last I was
getting to you. I was going to tell you I loved you and
see where that got me. Then I came back and you'd
gone. I think I went a little mad—I remember Madame
Lefeuvre looking at me as if she wanted to send for the
psychiatrist. I swore for five solid minutes. Then I
calmed down enough to decide I'd fly to London, find
Philip, grind him to a pulp and then turn my attention
to you. What I was going to do to you wasn't very clear,
but I think it was going to end with you in bed with
me, whether you liked it or not.'

'Poor Madame Lefeuvre,' Helen grinned. 'I've no
doubt she thought the worst. She has such a melo-
dramatic streak. I expect she's been reading the English papers and waiting to read about my murder.'

'She nearly did read about it,' Drew assured her.

Helen ran her hand down the smooth muscular
curve of his spine. 'Brute,' she said, kissing his shoulder.

'Do you think Stephen would like a brother or
sister?' Drew asked with a teasing little grin.

Helen viewed him obliquely, her blue eyes gleaming. 'Whether he likes one or not, I think he's going to get one. You do realise I've never taken any precautions to make sure he doesn't, don't you?'

'I wondered,' Drew said with satisfaction. 'I'd like a girl next. I like girls.'

'I had noticed,' Helen said with the faintest snap. 'But so long as you confine your attentions to our little girls I shan't mind.'

He laughed softly. 'For the moment I'll confine my attentions to you.' His hand slipped to the warm fullness of her breast and he groaned. 'Darling.'

Helen closed her eyes. 'Yes, Drew,' she sighed as she recognised the inexorable rise of desire in him, and the mouth he claimed wore a smile of relaxed happiness.

The Mills & Boon Rose is the Rose of Romance

Every month there are ten new titles to choose from — ten new stories about people falling in love, people you want to read about, people in exciting, far away places. Choose Mills & Boon. It's your way of relaxing.

February's titles are:

SUMMER OF THE WEEPING RAIN by Yvonne Whittal
Lisa had gone to the African veld for peace and quiet, but that seemed impossible with the tough and ruthless Adam Vandeleur around!

EDGE OF SPRING by Helen Bianchin
How could Karen convince Matt Lucas that she didn't want to have anything to do with him, when he refused to take no for an answer?

THE DEVIL DRIVES by Jane Arbor
Una was in despair when she learned that Zante Diomed had married her for one reason: revenge. How could she prove to him how wrong he was?

THE GIRL FROM THE SEA by Anne Weale
Armorel's trustee, the millionaire Sholto Ransome, was hardly a knight on a white horse — in fact as time went on she realised he was a cynical, cold-hearted rake . . .

SOMETHING LESS THAN LOVE by Daphne Clair
Vanessa's husband Thad had been badly injured in a car smash. But he was recovering now, so why was he so bitter and cruel in his attitude towards her?

THE DIVIDING LINE by Kay Thorpe
When the family business was left equally between Kerry and her stepbrother·Ross, the answer seemed to be for them to marry — but how could they, when they didn't even like each other?

AUTUMN SONG by Margaret Pargeter
To help her journalist brother, Tara had gone to a tiny Greek island to get a story. But there she fell foul of the owner of the island — the millionaire Damon Voulgaris . . .

SNOW BRIDE by Margery Hilton
It appeared that Jarret Earle had had reasons of his own for wanting Lissa as his wife — but alas, love was the very least of them . . .

SENSATION by Charlotte Lamb
Helen's husband Drew had kept studiously out of her way for six years, but suddenly he was always there, disturbing, overbearing, and — what?

WEST OF THE WAMINDA by Kerry Allyne
Ashley Beaumont was resigned to selling the family sheep station — but if only it hadn't had to be sold to that infuriating, bullying Dane Carmichael!

If you have difficulty in obtaining any of these books from your local paperback retailer, write to:

Mills & Boon Reader Service
P.O. Box 236, Thornton Road, Croydon, Surrey CR9 3RU

The Mills & Boon Rose is the Rose of Romance

Look for the Mills & Boon Rose next month

THE MATING SEASON by *Janet Dailey*
When Jonni Starr got engaged, she thought she ought to go
back to tell her parents. So back she went, and promptly fell
in love with another man . . .

LOVE IS THE HONEY by *Violet Winspear*
Iris agreed that it was time she found out what life was like
outside of her convent. So she went to work for the over-
whelming Zonar Mavrakis — and found out with a vengeance!

SPIRIT OF ATLANTIS by *Anne Mather*
After the shock of her father's death, Julie was having a rest-
ful holiday in Canada. Restful? Not with the disturbing Dan
Prescott around!

THE GOLDEN PUMA by *Margaret Way*
The abrasive David Hungerford thought that Catherine ought
to leave her father to make a life of her own. But what life
was there, without David — who wasn't interested in her in
that way?

MAN OF ICE by *Rachel Lindsay*
Happy to accept a job with the kindly Miss Bateman, Abby
found that she had brought on herself the contempt and
suspicion of her employer's dour nephew Giles Farrow.

HOTEL JACARANDAS by *Katrina Britt*
Julie's sadness over her parents' divorce was nothing compared
to her heartbreak when she fell in love with Felipe de Torres
y Aquiliño — who didn't want her . . .

THE FIRST OFFICER by *Anne Weale*
Four years' separation had not lessened Katy's love for her
husband. But Charles had been disillusioned by her once —
had she reason to suppose she had any attraction for him
now?

NIGHT MUSIC by *Charlotte Lamb*
'I bought you, and what I buy stays bought, even if it proves
to be worthless,' Steve Crawford told Lisa. Would she be able
to change his opinion of her?

DANGEROUS MARRIAGE by *Mary Wibberley*
Shelley knew nothing about the overbearing and mysterious
Vargen Gilev except that she loved him — and he did not
love her . . .

YOURS WITH LOVE by *Mary Burchell*
Virginia had fallen in love with Jason Kent as a result of
playing 'the other woman' in a plot to get rid of Jason's wife.
But how could Virginia go on caring about a man as selfish as
he was?

Available March 1980

If you have difficulty in obtaining any of these books from
your local paperback retailer, write to:

Mills & Boon Reader Service
P.O. Box 236, Thornton Road, Croydon, Surrey, CR9 3RU

Mills & Boon Classics

The very best of Mills & Boon
romances, brought back for those of
you who missed reading them
when they were first published.

in
February
we bring back the following four
great romantic titles.

THE CASTLE IN THE TREES
by Rachel Lindsay

The very name of the Castle in the Trees fascinated Stephanie,
and the reality was even more intriguing than she had imagined.
But there was mystery there too. Why did Miguel and Carlos
de Maroc hate each other? Stephanie found out at last, but
only at the cost of losing her heart.

ISLAND OF PEARLS
by Margaret Rome

Many English girls go to Majorca for their holiday in the secret
hope of meeting romance. Hazel Brown went there and found
a husband. But she was not as romantically lucky as she
appeared to be — for Hazel's was a husband with a difference ...

THE SHROUDED WEB
by Anne Mather

For several very good reasons Justina wished to keep the news
of her husband's death from her frail, elderly aunt. Then she
heard of the Englishman Dominic Hallam, who was in hospital
suffering from amnesia, and the germ of an idea came into
her mind ...

DEVIL IN A SILVER ROOM
by Violet Winspear

Margo Jones had once loved Michel, so when he died she found
herself going to look after his small son in the French chateau
of Satancourt. There Margo met Paul Cassilis, Michel's
inscrutable brother, to whom women were just playthings,
but in "Miss Jones" was to find one woman who was determined
not to be.

Doctor Nurse Romances

and February's
stories of romantic relationships behind the scenes
of modern medical life are:

NURSE ON WARD NINE
by Lisa Cooper

It was a wrench for Claire Melville to leave home —
and Martin — to nurse at the Princess Beatrice
Hospital, and on Ward Nine she encountered hazards
she had never expected — not least that cold-eyed,
moody Doctor Andrew MacFarlane!

SATURDAY'S CHILD
by Betty Neels

Saturday's child works hard for a living .... And so
did Nurse Abigail Trent, plain and impoverished and
without hope of finding a husband. Why did she have
to fall in love with Professor Dominic van Wijkelen,
who hated all women and Abigail in particular?

Order your copies today from your local paperback retailer.

Choose from this selection of
Mills & Boon
Golden Treasury
COLLECTION

ORDER NOW FOR DIRECT DELIVERY

- [ ] **GT51**
  COME BLOSSOM-TIME, MY LOVE
  Essie Summers

- [ ] **GT52**
  WHISPER OF DOUBT
  Andrea Blake

- [ ] **GT53**
  THE CRUISE TO CURACAO
  Belinda Dell

- [ ] **GT54**
  THE SOPHISTICATED URCHIN
  Rosalie Henaghan

- [ ] **GT55**
  LUCY LAMB
  Sara Seale

- [ ] **GT56**
  THE MASTER OF TAWHAI
  Essie Summers

- [ ] **GT57**
  ERRANT BRIDE
  Elizabeth Ashton

- [ ] **GT58**
  THE DOCTOR'S DAUGHTERS
  Anne Weale

- [ ] **GT59**
  ENCHANTED AUTUMN
  Mary Whistler

- [ ] **GT60**
  THE EMERALD CUCKOO
  Gwen Westwood

ONLY 50p EACH

SIMPLY TICK ☑ YOUR SELECTION(S)
ABOVE THEN JUST COMPLETE AND
POST THE ORDER FORM OVERLEAF ►